BOUNCE OVER

EXPECTATIONS

Spectrum Of Thoughts

AM/56, Basanti Colony, Rourkela, 769012, Odisha

An Affiliate Of FanatiXx

Website :- www.sotpublication.com

Published by Spectrum Of Thoughts 2022
Copyright © Shefali shireen, Harini Golaja, Heba naaz 2022
All Rights Reserved.

ISBN : 978-93-5452-903-0
Typesetted By: Mayuri Valanju
Cover Designed By: Sagar Samal

ACKNOWLEDGEMENT

First and foremost, we would like to thank the Almighty for the reason we are here today.

We thank every soul who helped us to bring this book a successful one.

We thank our head Kirti Aggarwal and Divya Renwa for giving us an opportunity and also for their constant support till the completion of the project.

We thank Spectrum of Thoughts Publication team for providing this wonderful platform for me and the budding writers.

We thank all the Co-Authors of this Anthology for being patient and keeping faith in us; co-operating, supporting and encouraging us in every step while making this Anthology.

We would like to give our heartily thanks to the Designer, Sagar Samal for giving such a wonderful cover page for this Anthology.

We also thank the Book Interior Designer for making the book a beautiful one.

DISCLAIMER

This Anthology is a melody of memories. The writers have beautifully described their every emotion through their write-ups and they have given their words that the write-ups are free from plagiarism.

So, if any plagiarism is detected in the book neither the publishing house nor the compiler will be responsible

SHEFALI SHIREEN

(Compiler)

Shefali Shireen is a software engineer working in an IT company. However, her favourite pastime habit since childhood was reading and writing it in her version. Her main strength is her friends and family who always supports and believe her in every step of her life without them she feels incomplete. She resumed her passion towards writing and displays her thoughts through posting quotes in

YourQuote   : Shefali Shireen (smartshireen)
Instagram ID : @shireen_smart

HARINI GOLAJANI
(Compiler)

Harini golajani is a budding writer at spectrum of thoughts publication. She currently pursuing b.tech. she hails from from Visakhapatnam. In free hours she likes to watch movies

INSTAGRAM: @harini_golajani

HEBA NAAZ
(Compiler)

Hi.. I'm Heba naaz. I like to write and the best way for me for an escape from every mess is by creating. I would like to write my feelings through my words.

rosy_naaz146@IG

HARSHITHA KHANDELWAL

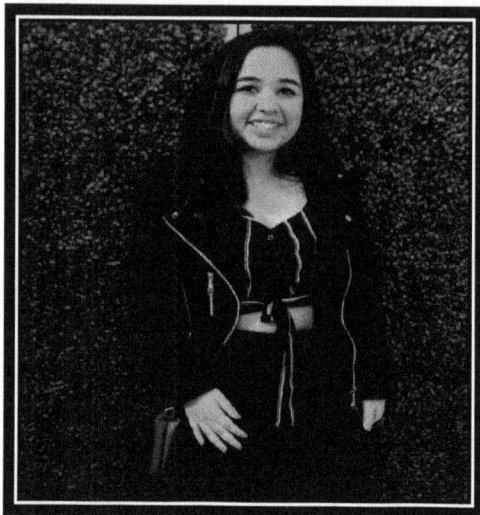

Harshitha Khandelwal, a software engineer, has always been highly enthusiastic of art and poetry. She draws, Photographs, dances, loves to talk. Music is a driving force for her. Keen on adopting a dog and trying to convince mom is a part of her daily muse.

Instagram ID : @learnyoursoul.

Void

I am scared of knowing it all,
feeling it all,
so I run away,
trying to catch my breath calming the racing heart rate.

Locked in dark rooms,
I try to make myself home,
in the closet I'm hiding.
I wish you held me closer mum
and that was not the only memory of you.

but whenever I think of warmth
I only remember your touch I crave you,
So, I stand below hot showers and feel your heat,
blankets and hoodies are my favourite pieces of fabric for they remind me
of you.

but then I see dad
trying to make breakfast
like how you did feeding me as he completes his online meetings
walking me to my prom
and attending my bakery sapphire.

It hurts sometimes
to miss you around and not find you.
a void in my heart
is still a void.
but the heart is still a heart too,
and its making space for new.

I didn't expect a new mum in my dad
but what I have is
the best I have ever had as I fall asleep in arms of two
I didn't know realities would reward me higher.

- Harshitha
Khandelwal

To My Younger Self

You want to be someone's muse,
like a river that flowers the paths,
It wanders,
leaving no parts untouched of the beauty.
You are an incomplete letter,
waiting for words to describe your abundant love.
the one you want to Pour into someone's soul.
but you forget you carry profound fertility and
Wholeness even if you don't reach the paths and fulfil them.
 And you are your own muse too.

You want to be someone's favourite song.
like a tune that they can't get out of their head
the music that keeps them warm.
Where they find symphony in the syncing.
but you forget that you are an entire playlist.
the songs that span across boundaries.
never one, never enough.
You want to be someone's home.
where someone can rest their heads
and just dance to your grace.

For what you can provide
spans beyond the physical space.
the soul that you find comfort in
that's now known to be a hiding space.
but you forget that you are your home too.

You want to be someone's favourite painting,
with every stroke they draw you feel the rush
the love that inks
the colours that bleed.
You want all of that.
and you will always remain the spectrum on canvas
as long as you believe
that you are the colours and the blood is yours.

maybe you don't realise

but your expectations
were excelled by the realities
that purely exist in the blur line of
what is yours will always be what you truly desire.

you look at the biggest of things that you expect
yet live for the tiniest of the details.
and those tiny things are your realities.
you are fuller and carved with more details than you think.
it might seem that you are drowning in the realms
but my darling you are transcending.
and to transcend,
you immerse.
and accept everything with grace and badges.
the cuts and stitches.
the glory and the mess.

- *Harshitha Khandelwal*

ROMI DEY

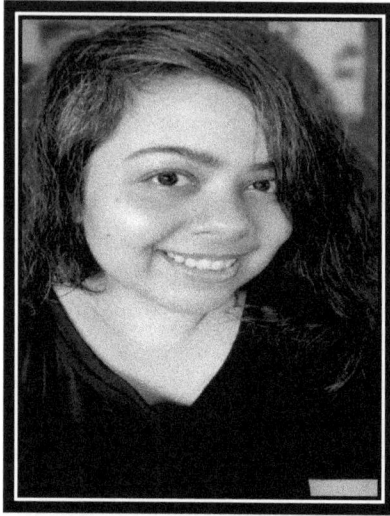

Romi is a design and writing enthusiast, alumnus of National Institute of Design, a traveller by passion and has keen interest in animals, spirituality, psychology and meditation. Based in India, she prefers to live a life of minimalism & simplicity.

Love

I feel I should start with Love.

Too soon? Isn't it?
Maybe it is. But that's exactly how it happens.
In a jiffy, in a moment, in a cup of coffee. And you fall in love.

I always felt and always knew I'm a person who can love easily and can
fall in love with anyone around her.
I have always believed in love.
You try and see the good part of a person around you. You start thinking
and imagining the person to be the
nearest one to your heart. You start prioritizing his or her life over yours.
That's love? Is it?

Somebody said to me once, love is just a feeling, a combination when
your hormones and your neuron talk to each other.

He said, we were similar in thinking, in being emotional and vulnerable.
He uttered the word "love" to me, in a different way though, but that was
the first time somebody said it to me.
The very first time in my entire life.

How could I not fall for that?
First time, I felt connected. Once again. After so many years, so many
fucking years!
First time, I felt, there exists a carbon copy of just me, in another part of
the world.
We were nearer though. Hence we decided to meet.

We met. We talked, chatted, ate, together. We worked together too. And I
decided, I'll say those words to him, one day and I knew that day will
come soon. And, I smiled.

-Romi Dey

Smile

The toughest curve I won't mind crossing every day.
The path I would like us to take all the while.
The magic that can happen to anyone.
That's smile.

I smiled, and I wrote back to him, I liked you.
"I liked you so much in these few days and I knew nothing about how..."

He said, "I like you too, as a person"

I smiled.
I felt magic. I witnessed love. I realized, that's him.

A smile can indeed do wonders. When someone smiles at you, and you smile back. When you expect someone to smile at you, and someone else smiles back...

Well, that's life.

"I have shared too much with you already, and this is something I haven't done in a long time!"

I smiled again. It's happening, isn't it God?

"Let's meet tomorrow at Park Street, we'll booze"

Made me smile again, once again. Then I thought, to myself,

"Are you ready, girl?"
"This is what you wanted; this is it!"

So, I wished.

- Romi Dey

Wish

I wished he wasn't married.
I wished I could get one chance of being together.
I wished I didn't face the reality too soon.

"<message deleted>"
   "Now, what did you delete?"

"I need to tell you something and I feel I should have told you earlier."

"What??? Tell me now!"

"I am married …"

Yet, I wished I didn't know it. But can we really control what's real? Can we really surpass what's evident? Guess we can't. Certain incidents in our life will keep on happening even if we don't need it or want it. You'll feel like you're in a big trap, called life, and you'd have just zero control on it. That's the power of wishes. Once we wish whole heartedly, with our crystal-clear intent, your wish would come true. For sure, at least for once it will hold true.
We'll keep wishing more. We'll keep imagining we belong to a beautifully perfect world and we'll never stop wishing.

   "Okay! That's Okay"

"Thanks God! You didn't react to it!"

And, I thanked God.

- Romi Dey

Thanks

Thank you.
 A small gesture, simple enough, casual, deep, filled with emotion.
Probably the only way to communicate how grateful you really are.

Thanks, we started working together, I got a chance to know him, the
person he is. The raw emotions that he carries, he possesses.
How could a guy be so emotional?
How could someone be this genuine?
Am I wrong in understanding him?
Or, should I simply thank God, he gave me this chance in life?
The more I interacted; I learnt, his intentions,
His will power,
His Genuinity,

We decided, we'll create together.
A new space,
A new design,
A new emotion,
Called,
Respect.

- Romi Dey

ABDULLAH AHMAD

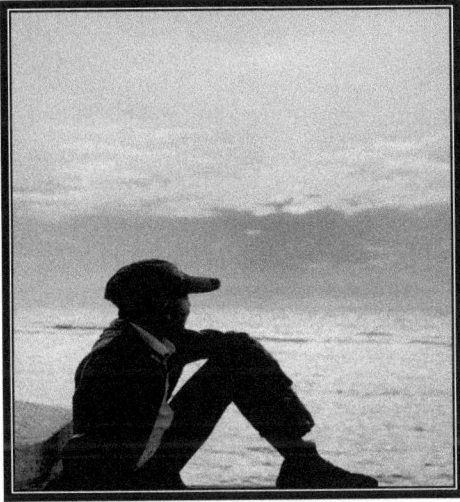

ABDULLAH AHMAD. A boy who lives with his head in the clouds but is still self-aware. A sensitive soul who can sympathize with anyone who crosses his path, Abdullah, besides writing, holds an attachment to cars and football.. He enjoys thrilling experiences and attributes this to the freedom that came with driving a car alone for the first time as a boy. Maybe some of this reflects in his words. You can find him engrossed in making edits for his Instagram page @_akaftblboi or bounding through the virtual archives of other poets before him, inspired by their words..

Imaginations Don't Always Stand Up To Reality

Once upon a time, I had gone to see a very Noble university (AMU). I had heard many stories about this place so I felt I had a clear image of what the place looked like. So once I decided to go to the university. I was thrilled, when I entered I felt like I was not in the right place because the image my mind had was totally different. Soon I settled, and realized how sometimes your imaginations can be very distinct from reality.

- Abdullah Ahmad

First Day of School

So it was the first day of school and to say the least I was quite excited, I had seen the building multiple times, though I had never experienced the inside. Soon the day came, I went to school and I wasn't in much surprise as I felt I knew how the place was. I realized that sometimes imaginations can be reality and sometimes they also might not exactly be.

- Abdullah Ahmad

The New Airport

I used to travel to different places once or twice a year. The airport through which I used to depart hadn't been changed and was basically untouched for several years until a few years back when a completely new airport was built. Soon I was traveling and arrived at the airport, I was stunned with what I saw! I had seen many videos but when I was there myself I saw so many more things which I did not imagine. It felt like a dream to say the least.

- Abdullah Ahmad

The New Bus

So it was just a normal day, I was going to the bus stop to catch my bus to go to the school, when I arrived my bus was nowhere to be seen but there were a few new buses. I felt that the buses might've been changed so I asked the people over there and it turned out I was certainly right. It felt good to have a change

- Abdullah Ahmad

KERRYANNE BROWN

Kerryanne is a keen writer and scientist. Science is the love of her mind, poetry is the love of her heart. Having only been writing for 2 years, Kerryanne is currently working on her first book.

Follow her work online:
Instagram ID : @kayabeecollection

Tainted Rainbow

Soft and fluffy the rainbow feels.
Held up by clouded slippers.

I glide along the brightly coloured path.

Rain drops hit my icy cold skin,
The sun feels warm upon my face.

I gaze upon the world like heaven.

Cracks begin to emerge in my mind,
Dark black holes follow.

I rock myself here, within the church.
Masks and wires, my chest is alive,
Warn and broken above me it stands,
The stained glass window.

- Kerryanne Brown

Unexpected End

Waking up tired and croaky,
I pull myself from my bed.
My feet touch the hard wood floor,
Head is fuzzy and unwired.

Today is a day,
The same as the last,
Everyone and everything,
Flying around fast.

But right now, it succeeds,
I see a message it reads,
"Come see me, 8:00 okay?"
Oh, what an unexpected day!

- Kerryanne Brown

The Tree

Anastasia sat and admired the tree as a child. It was so grand and quaint and giving.

It gave her mind peace. The leaves glistened in the morning sun, her eyes sat and wondered what the flecks of light could be, and where they could go after the tree bounced life back into them.

Once grown, Anastasia decided she would get her own tree, the same tree, a tree she could walk to and ponder. It would listen to her thoughts and desires.

She planted her seedling, and waited. Waited for it to grow and dazzle and shine.

Days came and went, the tree was the same. It was dull and boring and small. It was not the tree she desired, she perhaps thought to destroy, to rebuild.

Time past, she forgot, and the tree remained. Until one day, fruit began to sprout from the dense ugly leaves...berries, black juicy berries!

Beautiful berries, filled with taste and zest and hope. Anatastia sat at her tree, with a berry to her tongue, flecks of light shone through her eyes, with a child like energy once more. She sat, she pondered, she desired...she thought.

- Kerryanne Brown

The Dream

I dreamt last night that it was so,
I lost you when, you wished to go.

It was so sad, so unexpected.
I thought our love was so connected?

We fought and we cursed.
Cried and dispersed.

I awoke in a flutter,
My mind all a'splutter.

But I turned, you were there,
Eyes closed, not a care.

How real it seemed?
The dream, I just dreamed.

- Kerryanne
Brown

Dishonest Love

I gave in, gave you all of me.
You twisted our love for all to see.
You took my soul within your stride,
Destroyed my innocence with joyful pride.

You took me to the highest hill,
Made me laugh, and sing until,
You grabbed my hand, tighter still,
And lied to me, against my will.

- Kerryanne Brown

CHRISTOPHER FENN

Christopher Fenn has aspired to be a published writer since he was ten years old. Christopher began writing his own comic series, Seron, and has been nominated for 'Best Single Issue Unproduced Comic Book Script' in the Steelkilt Media Festival for his script writing.

Twitter   : @seroncomic
Instagram ID   : @seroncomic @seronwrites

Normal Norman

Norman considered himself normal. He didn't stand out much, really. Just a regular man doing regular things in a regular way.

Normal worked in finance. He never really dreamed of it; his childhood fantasies were not filled with spreadsheets or compound interest, but this was the line of work he fell into. Sometimes Norman wanted to leave. He would often think "what if I just went to Hollywood?", or "I'll just make it big on TikTok or YouTube!", but Norman never chased these dreams.

In fact, they weren't his dreams, they were the dreams he felt he was supposed to have. These were the dreams of the Zoomers... or was it the Millennials? Maybe they were the dreams of Gen Z, but aren't they just Zoomers? Norman wasn't too sure whose dreams they were, just that they weren't his.

When Norman thought of his own dreams, he thought of things like "having a nice curry whilst watching that film he wanted to see but, missed it when it was on at the cinema". He knew they weren't exciting dreams, and he knew for certain nobody would ever put them in a book, but they were his dreams.

Today was not the day for dreams, though. Today was the day Norman was going to get that promotion.

Norman didn't think he was particularly good at his job in finance. He started working for a bank when he dropped out of college. They were taking on and he knew that he could learn to make coffee and photocopies. Over time he managed to work his way up. His promotions always came way after his other colleagues, but he was okay with that.

It had been a few years since his last promotion, and all his work mates moved on to different teams. His oldest workmate, Steve, was applying to be a director, and Dave was head of some department or other. All that was left on Norman's team was him and a bunch of interns; kids straight out of university. Norman felt quite sorry for them. They must have got paid a lot less than him to do the same thing he had been doing for a while. That was just the way the world seemed to work now, and there was nothing Norman, or the kids, could do about it.

Norman had gotten an email late last week for a meeting with his manager, bright and early on Monday morning. He was quite lucky to have seen it, usually Norman just deleted his work emails. "If it's something important, they'll email me back!" he always thought.

"Norbit, the boss will see you now." Said the secretary. Norman always thought she was a bit rude, and she never got his name right. After the third time trying to correct her, he just gave up. Norman stepped into his manager's office. It was a big room, much bigger than Norman's little cubicle. His manager was working on his computer and instructed Norman to sit down.

"You're probably wondering why you have been called in here?" Norman's manager asked.

"Is it about my promotion?" Norman said, with more enthusiasm as he thought could be possible on a Monday morning.

"No, son," Norman always thought it was weird his manager called him son, considering Norman was two years older than him. "we're letting you go."

"It's just the way the world works now." Norman's manager continued, without looking up from his computer screen. "I wish there was more I could do, but my hands are tied."

"We wish you best of luck with your future career path." Norman's manager concluded, in a very monotone and unfeeling way.

"You too." Said Norman, whilst cringing, as he immediately knew this was a very stupid thing to say. His chair squeaked against the floor as he left. As Norman left the office, he realised that he could be anything he wanted. "Well," he thought, "not quite anything."

The first thing Norman ever wanted to be, as a child, was a Dinosaur, but in the current job market the prospects of this being successful was unlikely. The second thing he ever wanted to be was an ice-cream man. Kid Norman thought that he would be able to have all the ice cream and red sauce he wanted, and that was something that made everyone happy. There were a few hiccups with this; Norman had no savings to buy an ice-cream van, and Norman did not know how to drive.

As the walk from Norman's old office to home continued, his hopes of being anything got smaller and smaller. A bleak realization fell on Norman; he would end up back in finance somewhere else for far less money.

This would be a job for the Norman of tomorrow. The Norman of today was going to follow his dreams. He was going to sit on his sofa. He was going to order a curry. He was going to watch that film he wanted to see but missed when it was on at the cinema.

He opened his takeaway app and found his favourite curry. He even treated himself to a naan. Then his payment was declined. "Insufficient funds".

- Christopher Fenn

Dinosaurs Still Rule the World

Dinosaurs once ruled the world.

They ran across planes and dominated the land, seas and sky.

Their teeth and claws were the mightiest weapon. None could oppose their will or control.

They met a quick and sudden end. We are unsure if it was by fire or ice, but regardless their end was inevitable. Dinosaurs still rule the world.

We see their footprints across our roads. Their thick, black blood drown our oceans. Their smoky, black wings pierce our skies.

No longer do they have teeth and claws, however their remnants cause immeasurable death across the globe.

Though their end has come and gone, they tirelessly work to bring about ours. The thinning atmosphere, the scorching heat and their melting fury will bring about our undeniable extinction. Dinosaurs still rule the land. The extinct predator that cannot be stopped.

- Christopher Fenn

H.M. OLSEN RED SHOE POETRY

H.M. Olsen writes soulful poetry from the deep depths of a feminine heart. Her work has touched the hearts of many people around the world.. It has provided many women an understanding of what is moving deep inside of them. She loves to touch hearts, and her poems are often met with genuine tears from her readers

Tonight I Wanted To Write a Poem For You

Tonight I wanted to write a poem for you
But I was completely dumb
From all the years of your fingerprints on my heart
So devastatingly numb
I still sometimes turn to look behind me
In the cold autumn morning winds
I turn just one last time to see
Feverishly looking for your face
On all of these foreign streets
You always insisted never to hold my hand
Instead trying to hold my heart
In a golden cage on top of your dusty garage shelf
When reaching to hug me
On empty corridors of old abandoned shopping malls
You always walked right through me like a ghost
Like you knew you were already gone
Even if you were still here
I could never quite reach what I wanted with you
Death was a better contractor
Someone you finally dared to hold hands in public with
Court to fancy dinners
And dance to eternity
You were always so very, very dark, my lover
Too dark for my heart to see
So we ran past each other like two wild horses in the night
Never reaching your dreams
I will be someone else's fantasy now, my love.

- H.M. Olsen

Deep In the Night

Deep in the night
I stare at the ceiling of my room
Resting on the veil of remembrance
Touching the darkness with my heart

This darkness is safer
Than the darkness you brought into my life
Devilish nights with sweet burning lies
Always making me lose my way in the morning

Now, in the velvety soft blackness of this night
I am acutely aware of my safety
A tiny dancer in the dark
Spinning round and round and round
On an empty playground
Never reaching her dreams

I surrender, I whisper softly
You finally got me
As the misty night air slowly lures me towards sleep

I am working the long nightshift
To heal my creased, blinded heart
Beating like a shamanic drum in the deafening stillness of the night
Still alive
Just barely

The sky is so very clear tonight
I wish you were here to see it
But you always had mud on your eyelashes
Worms in your heart
Even if your eyes were open
You could never really see

So here I am
Safely alone counting the stars
Paving my way into the new life
Filled with daffodils and lotus petals

Still, I will always remember you.

- H.M. Olsen

Dark Nights with You

Your sultry sins not letting me sleep
Your breath of thick black smoke not letting me breathe

In your house, never feeling safe
Even if your love was overflowing
Rushing like a wild wave over me
Providing deep pleasure just before pushing my head under the water
Blaming me for forgetting how to swim

In your house
Where my forgiveness was holding the roof up
Keeping your rain out
Letting your game commence

You always mastered the control of your emotions
just like your relationships
that always slipped like quicksand through your fingers
Leaving only devastation behind you

Your bride was the most beautiful you had ever seen
Almost unreal
Your eager efforts to sustain her resulting in faceless ghosts born from
emptied hearts
Your heart beating the hollow sounds of burial bells

Your beautiful stubborness and wild narcissism
Hidden under a naive childlike energy of fun and inconsideration
Your endless harem of options
Following your beautiful poems and art,
Your deceitful positive life advice posts
Sealed with your plastic smile
Will always leave you empty handed
Abandoned by self love
Ending up in empty screams in cold corridors

In the chess of life
You always dominated and lost so well
Wanting to drain and crush every lotus flower that came your way

Yes, they will remember you
Your surprised eyes and self-victimised never ending smiles
Piercing so many female hearts

Leaving your heart forever haunted by the one that got away

She will be your last sin.

- H.M. Olsen

RAMYA REDDY JONNALA

She goes by pen name Aaryahi. Was a writer since a year. Reality is what we have to live in so, started to write my heart out so can live peacefully. She is a mother to one.

You can go through her page
Instagram ID : @aaryahi_aru01.

Accepting the Life as It Comes

Sakshi was an average student at school. But her sister was a topper. Parents compared Sakshi with her sister regarding marks. Disappointed Sakshi felt low but accepted for what she is and knew that her way of understanding the subject is different from her sister.

In the process of growing up, Sakshi chose to live a life with the career she chose and decided to live with the person she loved the most.

Before she made this decision, she had already gone through a lot in her life. She made mistakes but learnt a lesson from every mistake and paved a path for her bright future. But as she is a slow learner, her fate turned upside down.

Sakshi's parents decided to marry her to a person who has more money and riches. Her parents decided so because they thought she would be happy with the riches and money.

Sakshi dreamt of something and in reality something else happened. Dreaming is not bad. It indeed a really good thing, in fact very useful for a bright future.

But living in a dream entirely without caring of what you have to do for that dream to come true will lead to an unending silence or sadness in our lives.

So always remember,
"When we have the dare to dream,
Have the courage to face the reality of life."

Sakshi once was a very good listener and became a non listener. Instead of listening, she started to think negatively of everything and started to shout at everything and everyone around.
She lost her peace of mind.
She became someone who she is not.
But soon she realised everything and started to live a positive Life like she used to before.

Sakshi realised that everything happens for a reason. Finally started to accept life as it came.

- Aaryahi

ARAVINTH

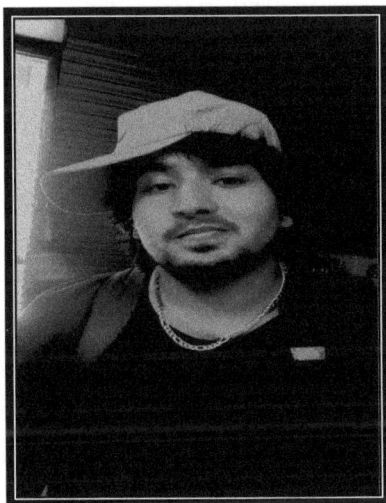

Billa is a budding writer, His Real name is Aravinth Sundaram. He is a Professional Athlete.He lives in the place called Erode in the State of Tamilnadu and completed B.Sc degree in Physical Education and sports science. Now he is Studying a Professional degree related to the Field of Sports. Writing Poems, Photography, videography, Editing and Listening Songs these are the hobbies of our Co-Author. "God's Plan" Is the first Short Story of Author BILLA

Instagram ID : @Poluthupoku_poet_go
Wattpad   : Billa Blogs

God's Plan

The Sun light kiss the fog; these teases make a birth to some Hail and Dew. On that Romantic morning inside the house, a couple Sameer and Rammy laying on the bed. Sameer awaken and kiss rammy's temple went to for planning espresso, suddenly rammy yelled Sameer!!!.... Aaaaa, Sameer!!!.... she began crying!!... Sameer fastly went into the room, He saw that Rammy crying because of her pregnancy torment, She conceded in the emergency clinic. it makes sameer a lot nervous and he is very frenzy about the introduction of their child. Out of nowhere the specialist call sameer and wear the activity dress and they permit sameer into the activity theater. Sameer have the undeniable degree of dread when he saw rammy laying on the bed With part of torment and battles, sameer haven't saw rammy like this ever at that subsequent he figures they don't need that child because he can't stand for the women he love suffer like a hell. He sense that he want to be with his beloved more than his child.

At last rammy have a glad labor, Yeah! They have female kid that time sameer have same glad drops on his eyes and bear his little princess on his hands Sameer saw his Queen's face and say she is appear as though you dear kiss her head. At that point sameer's affection unequivocally both the women and care them like his mother.

Rammy likewise love sameer as muchu he adores her. Around then the two of them are chosen to make a Naming Ceremony to their little princess. They fix a date for that service work everything is done rapidly, They consider everybody their companions, neighbours, family members and associates however they don't know about the name. Both are extremely befuddled to pick the name for their princess at long last they chose to named their minimal one as "SARA" (Gift from God). Sameer and Rammy's life went without a hitch and brimming with satisfaction after the Sara entered into their life. After certain months Sara grown up with charm and Naughtiness of the child's had, She is the world's greatest gift to the both sameer and rammy. Following not many days sara's feet kiss the ground and move the initial step of her life.

After she grown up quickly and a similar time her Naughtiness additionally experience childhood with her. Sameer and rammy are make sara as an autonomous disposition young lady Sara's folks gave full opportunity to her to do anything. She do all the experience exercises start like a men from 16years and she makes some Asian records moreover. After that she needs to compose his very own book. She is daring lady and I'll find any point to do in my life, this sort of a youthful gifted young lady. Her folks pleased to have a young lady like her and they believe she have most prominent future, At time rammy knows an aggravation on her lower stomach, definitely! you are correct she have a fantasy about their kid. She yelled more and Sameer came and take her to the medical clinic, Rammy was conceded on the crisis ward. The specialist said she is on muddled because she is pregnant and influenced by uterus cancer growth. After 3 hours battle between the specialist's and rammy. Around then sameer has no heart beats he thinks the 3hours he lives in the damnation that a lot of worsted time he has, The specialist open the entryway and said to sameer go to her lodge. The specialist said to sameer "Your significant other rammy has a disease tumour her uterus, Know it's taken out the activity is achievement, however she couldn't convey a kids". Sameer was broken to hear this word from the specialist's mouth. He completely disdain as long as he can remember yet the affection on her better one rammy is doesn't lose.

After certain weeks rammy realize that she couldn't conveying a child. She was as a rule extremely discouraged and crying here and there because of this dark times. At long last she chose to offer separation to sameer and she said to his hubby about her choice, sameer got outrage and chide about her bologna choice. Following not many weeks after the fact,The couples are went out on the town to shop they completed their shopping and went an inn for ate. After the two of them are going to the vehicle leaving region they hear a 3years child's crying sound. The two of them proceeded to see the side when the sounds came, Yes an experienced ladies around

35 years she felt down and kicked the bucket. On her almost a 3 years of age female child's saw her mom's face crying continuously, around then Rammy life that child and rub her eye drops. After that Sameer consider police and handover the woman's passing body and they document a guarantee duplicate to having that female kids as their own child. Your thinking is correct, yes the lady has no family she remained street side tents such a pitiless heart to the God. After that the couples are penance their whole to the female kid and they named as Sara. At long last Sara is back.

In everyone story God has a plan, so don't expect as your visuals are make a sculpture.

Everything under the GOD'S PLAN

- Aravinth

SHIVANI DAVE

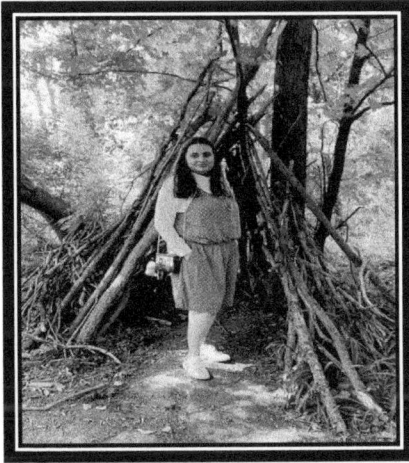

Shivani Dave is an emerging writer from India; currently residing in Canada with professional career in quality Industry. She believes in following the dreams; filtered by dream catcher! Her journey as a writer is moving forward one step at a time.

Follow her work on
Instagram /wattpad / twitter handle : shivani_jahnavi

Bouquet of Roses

Nihar always got me pink roses for special occasions. Today lying here in hospital bed; pregnant for almost nine months I'm waiting for a bouquet of pink roses more than him. Should I feel guilty; about the fact? Probably I shouldn't! Nihar will understand; he always does!

For every sweet instance of my life; or say our life I have been addicted to the honied soft smell of velvety petals and moisten air surrounding it.
Nihar has been that micro water droplet spread over the petal showering fondness amidst my life surrounded by thorn on the stem of that very rose flower I love!

There use to be a small rose plant in backyard of the orphanage I grew up! Lonely and unforeseen; nurtured without being sowed. I always had empathy with it; same like me nobody expected it and still we both exist!

I always found my solace with that tiny plant which grew up with me. We weren't welcomed or planted with prospects of growing up; and yet we did.
From what I hear around the place; my mother was a teenage drug addict and had me from one of her
one night stand and didn't even had money to abort me! So; she chooses to give birth and dump me at a random orphanage to look after myself!
Never in my life of eighteen years anyone came to inquire about me; and from the stories I heard; I
didn't have the heart to look for my mother!
The hardest part of leaving the orphanage behind was that wild rose plant in backyard; so, my friend
Nihar; who was leaving as well got me one flower from it for keepsake.
It's almost a decade; but I still have that single flower wrapped carefully in a transparent plastic cover; placed in wooden box as memento of my survival in all these years.
Life changed quite 360 degrees in last decade!
Nihar went from friend to best friend, lover to fiancé and now from husband to would be father of my girl.

When Nihar initially proposed the idea to be in relationship I was hesitant; I was not ready to lose the only friend and family I had throughout my life!

Nihar convinced me he will be the dew drop on my rose petal making me glow and spread my fragrance to surrounding making us happy; he will be an addition or multiplication to my life in any aspect I need him; but never be the subtraction and I had to agree after that poetic or rather mathematical explanation.

Looks like I'm in for a long wait for both my girl and her daddy. I came to hospital this morning as soon as I started having contraction.

It can be "Braxton-hicks" so I delayed calling Nihar until afternoon; he is out of town working to obtain new contract for our toy factory.

As soon as he heard I'm in hospital Nihar wanted to run back to his girls leaving everything behind; it was hard to persuade him; to finish work before coming.

While I'm in my random thoughts; my phone chimes alerting me of new message. I lean on my side to grab the phone from side table and see who it is.

Nihar ♡: Sweetheart; I'm leaving from here and see you as soon as possible; I hope our baby girl
waits for me to be at hospital before deciding to arrive in this world! Not calling because you might be resting! And just FYI... Meeting was successful! Take care..... love you, my rose! 😊
Message brought a bright and wide smile on my face; Nihar always addressed me rose when he is too excited or happy!
I replied him back with same overwhelming emotions...

Love 💋: Your girls can't wait to see you; but drive safely and don't forget my roses! Looks like our baby girl had already chosen sides; nurse just check up and told me it's still couple of hours more until I go into labor! She doesn't mind giving her mom a bit more pain and wait for daddy to be here! Also; congratulations partner for getting the contract; will join you back at work soon! I'm so proud of you for handling everything by yourself! I love you too Nihar! 😊

NIHAR
NIHAR
NIHAR!!!

I started shouting angrily; Nihar, wait for me...
How can you run in the rose field without me? Don't you know how much I love; them and you? I want
to enjoy this moment where my eyes behold so many roses and you in the same frame!
Don't run away from me...

Finishing my sentence, I put forward my hand for Nihar to take in his own!
But why is he not listening to me?
That has never happened before; Nihar is always there for me even before I get a chance to call him!
And today somehow; he seems to be going afar; without looking back; alone!
Suddenly the warmth of roses disappears and coldness of the thorn envelopes me; making a shiver run through my body.
Why can't I see Nihar anymore? What's with this stupid foggy vision? Why am I crying?

NIHAR
Nihar
Nihar
nihar....

My voice is muffled now; I cannot even hear myself.
When I open my eyes suddenly a ray of strong light penetrates inside, and I closed it again!

I don't want to open them but something is telling me I should face the light again; accept the reality!

When I slowly open my eyes again, I see white; even the clothes of people around me, walls, light, the bedsheet I'm lying in; every freaking thing visible is white!
Why; white? When I'm fully awake I comprehend that I'm still in hospital but in different room than earlier!
There is a nurse standing near the head of my bed holding a clip board and writing something; when she notices I'm awake she gives me a bland pitiful smile as if I'm someone with misfortune.

Well; I was before but not anymore! Since; I met Nihar on that rainy night in backyard of orphanage in the witness of my rose plant; my life changed for good!

Nihar was my first and only friend; and now my everything!

Wait; but where is Nihar? He messaged me he will be here soon before our baby girl arrives in the world! Wait; why I'm not feeling anything?

When I placed a hand over my belly covered with the same boring white sheet, I feel nothing; its flat!
Where is my baby girl?

I started panicking; hardly any words came out of my mouth; still I tried to ask the nurse in broken sentence; W-wherei-sss Nihar? Mmm-y bb-babby? What happened? Where am I?

Nihar

Nihar

Where are you?

I always like calling Nihar by his name instead of baby or darling or any meticulous or lovey-dovey pet names couples like to use.

Because saying his name; Nihar, every time it fills my heart with different volume of gratitude. It makes me realise whatever I suffered for initial decade of my life is worth it; if Nihar is there to fill in
the remaining years of my life!

The nurse doesn't answer me and goes out; maybe she will call Nihar and he will tell me where our baby girl is!

Oh god; I still don't know what is her name? Nihar, said he has already decided the name for our girl and

I'm to like it or rather love it very much but he will tell me about it after her birth; it's a surprise for me!

When the door opens, I expected Nihar to come in but instead the same nurse shows up again; followed

by other two white coat wrapped man; I suppose should be doctors here.

Confusion, worry, anger and frustration are taking over me; I was about to lash out at them but one of doctors out of the two; calls me and I suppress my outburst deciding to listen him out first before bombarding them with my questions.

Mrs. Nihar; how are you feeling?

Yes; I preferred being called that "Mrs. Nihar" it makes me feel more closer to him and as he doesn't
have last name just like me, being an orphan; we go by Mr. and Mrs. Nihar.
I contemplate internally but maybe my expressions says it all; Is he seriously asking; how I'm feeling? He continues when I don't respond rather glare at him for asking this stupid question instead of calling
my Nihar.

I know you have lots of questions but before that we need to know that you are fully awake and in right mind before telling you what happened during the week you were unconscious!

What? I was asleep for a week? And what happened? What is he talking about?

To get proper answers from them I believe I will have to open my mouth and answer them first so they
can finish off whatever it is and let me meet my angel and Nihar soon! With that thought I got up in the bed and asked with confidence; I'm fine just tell me where is my baby and Nihar?

Dear Sweetheart;

I love you! I know it's a most cliché thing to say; I love you and that to in a letter when I can say it to you 24x7 in person!
But somehow the talk about our baby girl always makes me an emotional mess; and I don't think I would be able to finish saying without crawling in my own tears and yours; which I definitely hate! I cannot see you crying even if its happy tears so I'm writing this down for you to read it and maybe after years lateryou can gift this to our angel and she will know how we named her.

When you will be reading this letter; I'm definitely sure our little angel might be asleep or playing with
me! You always told me; you liked my name! And I promised you I will always add to your life!

This is the best I could add to our life! Our little angel! A human being; a living proof of our love! Even
though I didn't have much contribution except one in creating this beautiful princess of ours; I would
take this opportunity to name her.

I didn't have any attachment with my name sweetheart; until you started calling it! Whenever you call me by my name, it makes me feel loved and wanted. From being a secret admirer to your husband the journey has been wonderful; and you were the only
one who made me feel accepted for what I'm am; in my whole life!

When I set down to write this letter, I was planning to write only about naming our baby girl; but don't know something tells me within to pour my heart out to you! I have never been much vocal about how much I love you or how much I treasure you and your

presence in my life! You have been an inspiration for that boy sitting near the window lost of any

perspective. You have been a friend to that teenager who doesn't know how to talk to people around.

You, my love; have been foundation to my very emotions of falling in love for the first time in life. You

have been amazing girlfriend to this stupidest boyfriend ever! You, my wife; yes, wife! it still feels surreal to call you that; have been the best partner a man can ever dream about! And now; I will be the luckiest to call you the mother of our child!

I am equally nervous and excited; but that's for me; not you! I'm sure you will be the best mom; to our little angel and her siblings in future!

Before I go to the main point of this letter; let me tell you this if I haven't been clear all this time!

I love you sweetheart; I'm grateful to God that I met you and I am thankful to you for staying; after

knowing this crazy-idiot of me! I'm the luckiest man alive and would be the happiest and most content

even if I die the next moment.

So; I thought of naming our baby girl "Niharika"!

You liked it?

I'm confident that you loved it actually!

If you did; come give me a kiss right now than read further!

I actually stopped mid letter and had to kiss Nihar! And just like first time I still have tears in my eyes as I am reading the only letter, he wrote me!

I guess I was worthy of that kiss after all! I named her "Niharika" for two reasons;

1. Because you love me and my name

2. I promised you addition and multiplication in life!

Our baby girl is the addition to our happiness and few extra letters in her name is multiplication to the love you have for my name!

Niharika; baby if your mom gave you this letter to read means your name was approved by her; also, she and I love you very much! We will always be proud of you; no matter what!

Rose

People saw thorn; but your touch was soft
as petal!
People saw strident; but your voice was lax
as pink!
People saw storm; but your charm was sweet
as nectar!
People saw mire; but your confidence was firm
as roots!
People saw autumn; but your love was foundation
as springs!

My Love;

People saw abandon; but your heart was warm
as zeal!

Love
Your Nihar!

Nihar; I gave your letter to Niharika today! It's her birthday; she is turning 25 today! Also, it's been same years since you left both of us without saying good bye and giving me my damn bouquet of roses but that I will settle when I meet you again!

I thought it's the right time! You know our little angel is now a big girl and would be joining our company soon! My days of retirement are near now!
I still miss you!
I love you Nihar!

When I turned back from Nihar's picture I saw Niharika crying her eyes out; holding the letter to her chest!
When our eyes met; she runs towards me and hold me in a tight hug saying; I love you mom! You are the best! Dad was right! And just like that few petals blew off from the rose by passing wind; but the thorns were still intact! Life is painfully beautiful without you *Nihar*!

- *Shivani Dave*

ANDY VINCK

The words of the wise man only reaches few.
Those with ears to hear, able to learn something
new.
The wisdom i give can be found within,
Not Knowing who you are, the original sin.
What you see with your eyes, a confusion of mind.
Listen to yourself, And A creator you shall find.

– Yodahz

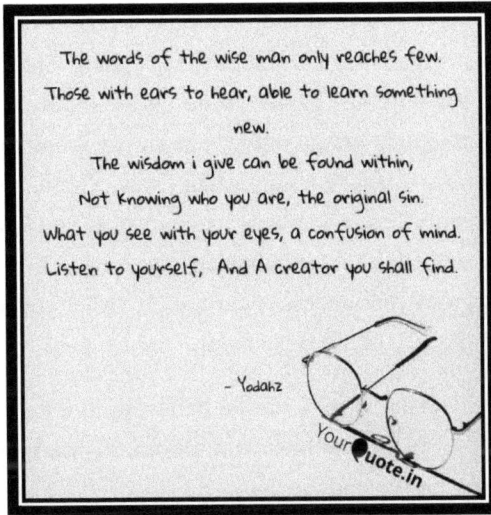

Andy aka Yodahz is a budding writer at Spectrum of Thoughts for Bounce over expectation. He hails from Limburg in Belgium. He enjoys helping and inspire people during his free hours.

You can find him and his poems at
Instagram   ID: Yodahz
Your Quote   : yodahz

A Story of Confusion and The Imagination

I want to share an experience I had when i was going through a confusing time in my life. My wife just gave birth to my firstborn. To whoever has not experienced this, this brings overwhelming emotions to pass through your body and mind. It was in a time when i was exploring consciousness and the relationship it has to the world around it. If you know something about religions and all the "enlightened" humans. There is always 1 concept that returns; "you are what you think", "what youeek you find" , "as within, so without", "as above so below" the list goes on and on.

To get back to my experience, i started believing in this, not only in my mind, but also in my heart. But there was always this doubt that stood next to it. To make you understand the complete story, i have to go back to my past, my Roots. I was a happy child, with AL LOT of imagination. I could create worlds within worlds, and keep track of them all. As i grew older i grew more attached to the outside world. Most of that was how other people saw "me". Then the time comes when a person starts to look for Love.

And when you find that all attachments fall from you like leaves from a tree in autumn. But then something happens you don't expect; you get humiliated and your trust gets broken multiple times. I can tell you, if that happens the first time you show yourself to a person you completely open up to, you are traumatized and lose trust in everyone for life, without even knowing it. It gets rooted in your subconscious so deep and it stays there.

Now back to my experience. I'm not really a jealous man. But like i mentioned i had trust issues.

As mentioned the birth o a child brings about alloy of emotions. The love you feel is overwhelming. And that love triggered something within me, that brought so much confusion. Because in deepest parts of my subconscious i learned that love will hurt you and humiliate you. It was at that time that i was deeply believing your thoughts ia. Imagination creates the world around you. But at the same time still doubting. There was all this confusion in my head, and it started to show itself in the world around me. I started to imagine, and believing my wife was cheating on me. Now my wife would never do something like that, that is why i wanted to have children with her. But without knowing it, i kept on believing it and imagine about it more. Now if i tell you that the stuff i imagined, presented itself to me in the world around me. But always with a sprinkle of doubt and confusion. You can call me mad or insane, but that is the sanest thing someone can believe in. I mean just look around yourself and what you are thinking about when you don't realize your thinking. I was in this "dream" for 4 years, it was circle that kept going on and on, i would imagine, over think and then something would happen which "confirmed" it. But looking back now there was always a logical explanation. But my expecting that i would find something brought it into being.

Although not in the way i believed. It was showing me in plain sight that what i imagine and think about manifests, although i was not focusing on that lesson, i was focusing on the doubts and confusion. I started realizing i needed to make a choice, accept the belief that she was cheating on me, or accept the belief that my imagination and expectations create my reality, fully without any doubts. I started to choose for the latter, altho it was difficult with constantly being pulled back to old habits of thinking. Until i started to make a new story, one where i see the love my wife gives to me and my children every day, where doubt and confusion did not exist. And sure enough after a couple of months the world around me started changing, again.. There were still moments the old world would try to slip in, but i gave those thoughts no attention at all, this is difficult but with enough will it can be done. Throughout this all i felt a strong pull to something within me, so i started to meditate again, something i forgot in my confusion. I started asking the question i was seeking on the outside, to myself in meditation. What i found was a feeling of love that i always thought came from something on the outside, and i realized this feeling is something you can have all the time.

So i started to focus myself on that feeling, and this is when my world changed forever.

I started to see love in everything, every person, in all of nature, every thought, they all have a reason. To remind you that whatever you hold in your heart, is what you will find the world. I started seeing the people who i could not stand, as a lesson to teach me, and sure enough those people changed how they acted to and infront of me. And more and more the connection with my truth grew stronger. When there where days when i felt low, i would remind myself there is always a lesson, and sure enough you will find it. Be it patience, love, tolerance, trust and once you find it, the situation will change. But if you don't you will fall into the dream and react to it, wich in turn will create another experience like it. Because if you don't learn the lesson, it will keep repeating itself, over and over like the circle I was in. I then started to get pulled into a direction in which i wanted to share all this and the knowledge i have learned. I started creating poems. Putting into words all that i know, and it all came so naturally. And since i am doing that, its like someone dictates what i should write, and i just put it down. And before i knew it, people started asking me to write books, anthologies. Like a leaf following the wind to wherever it pleases i accepted the offers. To be clear, i am not a religious person. I do not believe in a god on the outside because to me all religions talk about the same thing, teach the same lesson. But I do believe in a higher consciousness in each and all of us, and it talks through and to us in our imagination.

And we can work/ co-create with it by using our imagination and expectations. You can disagree with me, and I believe you will have reason to do so. Because that's the beauty of our free will, you get to choose what you believe; you get to choose what you imagine. And in turn you will experience what you believe in. So what is a truth for you, really is the truth, but for you alone.

- Andy Vinck

BIDYUT DEB

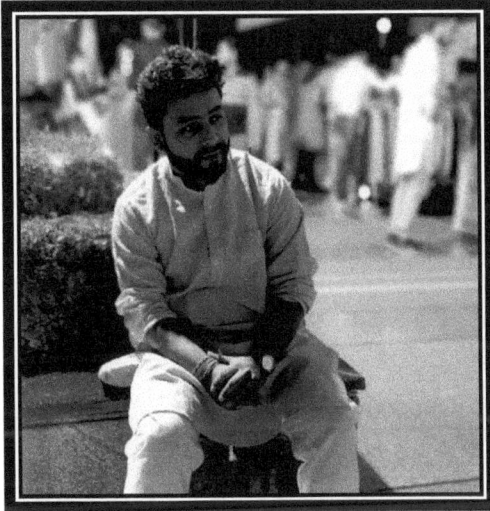

Bidyut deb is Working professional in a Gurugram based MNC, Born and raised in Meghalaya, Shillong, A Small hill station in the North Eastern part of India, He is a budding writer too and believes in putting his believes strongly, Co-founder of a dance group The passionatez, also likes to play flute, Writes ghazals and poetry's, also wants to make a significant contributions in reforming the society.

You can reach him on his instagram account
Instagram ID   : @shayar.dev_64

वजूद

ज़रा सा ग़ौर कर ध्यान दे
मेरी आँखों से वह असू टपके नहीं है अभी ,
वह जो बात होठों से करनी थी बया
हुई नहीं है अभी ...

वह जो सीने में टिस सा
उठा वह दर्द काम हुआ नहीं है ,
वह मेरे नफ़्ज़ ने दौर ना बांध
किया नहीं है अभी ...

वह मेरे नींदो से सपना छूटा नहीं है
वह मेरे बिस्तर से सिरहाना छूटा नहीं है ..

मेरे दोस्त मेरे हमदर्द
मुझे इस मीठी नींद से मत जगा ..

वह जो मेरे शहर में उठा वह
कोहराम थमा नहीं है ,
घरो का जलना ,
इंसानियत का मरना,
थमा नहीं है ...

वह जो लोगो के दिलो में दहशत
ख़तम हुआ नहीं है..

वह जो फितरत से मजबूर तानाशाह
हास रहे है कही,
वह जो अंधी भीड़ का हिस्सा है
जग रहे है कही ...

तू चुप रेह खामोश होजा
तेरी आवाज़ जो ख़ुदा भी सुनले
ऐसा कोई सोर्स नहीं है ...

मेरे क्या है

एक पागल सा शायर हु ,
लिखता रहा हु लिखता रहूँगा
इसके आगे तोह मेरा भी वजूद नहीं है ....

- Bidyut Deb

दास्तां

वह दिन भी कुछ अजीब था
वह रात कुछ और थी,
हम अकेले थे खरे
पर चारो और शोर थी।

था देखता में हर जगह ...
मुफलिसी करीब थी ,
खरा रहा उम्मीद पर
तू ही तोह वह डोर थी।

में नफरतो में था जला
तुमको भी तोह में खला
में पापी हु तोह क्या बुरा
तुम संत हो तोह क्या भला।

सिर्फ दास्तान मेरी नहीं
न नयी येन बात है
जो लेटा हु में कब्र में
तब तुम्हें सुकून है।

जिस्म मेरा मिटटी अब
रूह मेरी आज़ादी है
फिर भी जाने क्यों बंधा
झूटी रिश्तेदारी है।

ए खुदा कुछ ऐसा कर
लू जनम फिर धरती पर
में जहा था कल खरा
वह भी आएं हर कर
वह भी आएं हर।

- Bidyut Deb

जज़्बात

अक्सर सुना है
में अपने जज़्बात
बया नहीं करता।

ग़लतफ़मी है तुम्हारी
जो में बात नहीं करता।

बस हल ए दिल
बया करने का तरीका अलग है।

तुम बोलके समझते हो
और मुझे समझाने के लिए
बोलना नहीं परता।

- Bidyut Deb

कटघरा

आज फिर से उमीदो
के कटघरें में
तुमने हमको खरा कर दिया।

कुछ तुम भी रुस्वा हुए
कुछ हमको भी कर दिया। .

और भीगे है हम...
ऐसी कई बरसातों में
इक तेरी ही चुप्पी नै
हमको बीमार कर दिया।

पूछा न कोई सफाई हमसे
इश्क़ क पहरेदारो नै।

बस हल सुना उनका
और सज़ा हमको मुक़र्रर कर दिया।

- Bidyut Deb

PIYUSH PARTE

His name is Piyush Parte. He loves to write and learn new things He is a theatre artist and has also secured first position in martial arts at the national level. Apart from writing, he also enjoys to workout, drawing, acting, music, travelling and watching visual content.

Instagram ID   : @flavorsofwords

To Love

When I met you for the first time I didn't think that I would fall in love with you but it happened. I tried my best to stop myself but I couldn't stop when I first saw you I liked you your eyes, your face, your voice everything. The way you looked at me, talked to me, I felt very different, I had never felt that way.

I miss you, I miss you a lot every day I keep thinking of you. Whenever I go to a new place, I think how much fun it would be if you were with me. Do you know why I started writing poetry, for you because you like.

I am not a unique person, I am just a common man who has some dreams, I live a simple life, not many people know me and no more I claim that I will be successful in whatever I want to do, may be I fail.

But in only one sense, I am as successful as any other living being that I love you with all my heart. I know we never talked much but whatever we talked about was enough to love you.

I know that it is very difficult for both of us to live together and I also accept it but my mind does not believe it.

My mind thinks only about you. Every single bit of me wishes to be with you. I have never loved anyone the way I love you.

Your and only yours

-Piyush Parte

SRI VIDYA. G.R

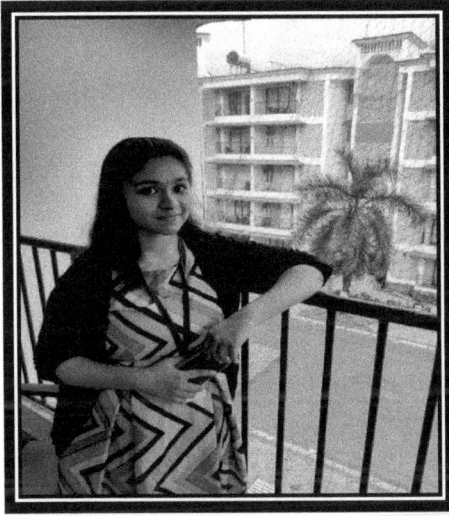

Sri Vidya.G.R, she has a great passion towards English since childhood. She is an eminent, young writer who usually loves writing poems with rhyme scheme. She is the rising writer.

You can refer her works in
Instagram ID   : @ sri_speaks,
Your quote   : Sri Vidya,
YouTube   : sri speaks grammar,
Mail ID   : srividyaganeshbabu@gmail.com

A Letter to YOU!

We all dream, we assume things, view in our own perspective and at the end of the day we EXPECT!

For what do we expect?
May be for our own betterment of life ?
For our closed ones' betterment?
Awaiting for someone's love? For health ,wealth,etc...
Whatever we wish whether it's good or bad , the ultimate thing is we expect. We expect to be fit , we wish our partner to show all their care , we wish to get good scores in academics, we wish to be recognised in whatever we do. Sometimes it sucks when the expected thing goes wrong in other way. Isn't it? When there is no satisfaction, we expect and we expect to get satisfaction.

But when the expected thing is undone we're downed.

-Sri Vidya

People and Their Prospects

When we do the things what we have to do, why should we expect?

Expectations won't let us live peacefully.

It starts from expectation and ends with frustration. We spoil ourselves and ruin our happiness by expecting things.

Expectations on people - question yourself "who are you? To satisfy your expectations on others?"

Whoever it may be even when it comes to your first circle! You can't always express things what you expect from them and that makes your bond unattached. And if you expect things on relationship there is no understanding between you is revealed. For example: You can't expect to revert back what and all you've done for them. Then think of this, what will happen when your parents starts expecting all the things back what they have done for you!!! Expectations in relationships will lead to chaos.

-Sri Vidya

Expectations of Others From You

It's not mandate to do things what others expect from you. But when it comes to your duty you're the only person to be answerable. Before they expect the duties , you should make them aware that you've done the things what should be done.

For example : when you are working under someone or when you do your schooling it's your duty to complete your tasks.

Secondly, you should never expect the appreciation for your works. Because you ll get what you really deserve. Some people appreciates on your face and some at your back . But your emotions should not connect other's opinion. You will be appreciated for your work directly or indirectly in the right time and place.

-Sri Vidya

Self Expectation and Appreciation

Self expectations are needed and that pushes you to go further. You should expect your best only if you've given your best.

But before expecting yourself, toil hard for the goal , achieve it and then expect the betterment of next time achievement.

When you are not appreciated, push yourself by patting your shoulders. In this world, appreciating others is rare and that sounds different now-a-days.

So just live every moment joyfully without any expectations on you, on others or on things.

-Sri Vidya

Expectations and Emotions

When a person is emotionally unstable, they start to expect things.
Be confident on yourself and on the relationships you travel with where you will not know what expectation is.
And when one is expecting things that you can't do, there is no need to get connected emotionally or feel bad. If it is possible, try to change their mind and bring hope for them on you.

Live the Life to the fullest without any expectation.
Lead the life with the heartful of satisfaction.
And that's our resolution.

-Sri Vidya

GARNET

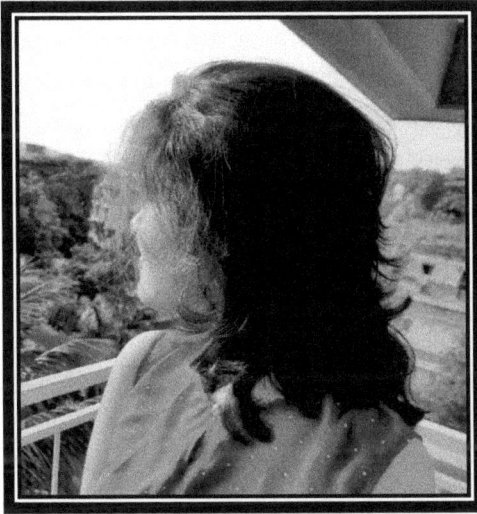

Garnet is your friendly neighbourhood writer. A software engineer by profession, she also enjoys reading, capturing the skies and is a proud Gryffindor. When she's not with a book or a pen, you'll find her catching up on the entire binge worthy movies and TV shows. Bounce over Expectation is her first venture into showcasing her work. Feel free to reach out to her:

Instagram ID : @lavender_carnations
Mail ID   : garnetwrit8@gamil.com

A Memorable Sunday

As a corporate professional, one thing I look forward to every week is the weekend. And I like to spend my weekends leisurely, reading a book or binging a TV series while eating my favorite food. So, it was a change of scenery when my mom suggested we go on a day tour to Velapur that was organized by our city's INTACH (Indian National Trust for Art and Cultural Heritage) chapter. As much as I love my relaxed weekend, I thought I needed to get out of the house. The trip was on Sunday and some of my friends decided to accompany as well. And so, the plan was set. On Sunday, we were officially going on a road trip.

But of course, things went downhill right from the very beginning. We were supposed to hit the road at 7 am and yet even at 7:30 there was no sign of the bus. We were an hour and a half behind schedule and then, our very own archenemy of road trips – rain – decided to make an appearance. When it stopped raining and we were on our way to the first site, I thought maybe things will look up now. We arrived at our first site which was an ancient temple and as beautiful as it was, it was surrounded by mud. Fresh mud, which made it a hundred times difficult to even walk, given that we were in a village.

And so, this went on up until the third temple and by this time my sister had gotten her head hit twice, courtesy of the old entrances and her 6 feet tall frame. We thought we might need to take her to a hospital, given the last door she hit was metal. By noon, I was starting to rethink my decision of going.

We finally arrived at the main attraction i.e., the 'Ardh Nari Nateshwar' temple at round 1:30 pm and I was stumped. It was beyond beautiful. By this time, the weather had also cleared up. There were also around 20 turtles that we saw in the water down by the temple, which resembled a pond. We explored the temple for a while, clicked photos here and there and it was time for lunch. We were served in a traditional Indian food setting and I am not exaggerating when I say it was one of the best meals I've had in a long time. And of course, good food lifts up the mood.

After lunch, we visited a collection of ancient stone inscriptions, we visited another lake side temple where the view was magical. We then clicked a lot of commemorative pictures and we were on our way home. We also surprisingly made it back not too late. As I got home, even though I was exhausted, I recalled the rollercoaster of events that had taken place. Even though the start had been rocky, we had made it and had a lot of fun. It was one of my most enjoyable experiences. And I am looking forward to many more of such impromptu, eventful and above all memorable experiences.

- Garnet

Memories That Were Never Made

Dear Student,

I've always been fascinated by the idea of college. Ever since I was a kid, I would dream about how awesome it would be, when I grow up and go off to college. I would be the cool student who rode their bike, who went out with friends, who bunked classes and yet aced the exams, who enjoyed in the cafeteria and what not.

As I watched my older sister go through with her college life, I couldn't wait to get out of high school. I would be able to do all that I had wanted to since I was a kid. And I had everything planned. The city, the college, the stream, the dorms, everything. But then Covid hit. I did complete my 12th Boards just in time before the 1st lockdown but now my future was uncertain.

I didn't know what my future education would look like, that is if I survive Covid first. I spent months assuring myself that everything would go back to normal by the time I needed to go to college. But it didn't. I did get into the college of my choice and I was happy. I thought even though there has been a delay, things will go back to normal.

I couldn't have been more wrong. I'm in my 2nd year of college now and I haven't even seen the campus, the classrooms, the cafeteria, the dorms, nothing. All the plans that I had made were in vain. All the memories that I had dreamed of, I couldn't make them. And I'm not going to lie, all of this was frustrating and disappointing, but I talked to my sister and she made me realize something.

I was still studying, more importantly I was alive, had a roof over my head, had internet and essential gadgets to attend the virtual classes. I had the privilege to sit at home relaxed and enjoy the classes. Eventually, I guess, I did come around. I may have never seen them in person, but I've made quite a few friends and we may not hang out in the cafeteria, but we do play 'Scribble' and 'Among Us' every other night. I may not have spent hours writing assignments and journals, but I have spent quite a few while drafting them online. I may not have bunked classes, but I did scroll through Instagram during lectures. I even attended a virtual Fresher's party.

My college life isn't what I had imagined, but it is rewarding in its own way. I may or may not ever see the actual campus, may or may not see my friends but that doesn't make it any less of an experience. On the contrary this experience is one that I am never going to forget. I mean, this period might be what students in the future have in their history textbooks; and they will probably be in awe of this generation. In the end, what I've learned from the past two years is that, you might have everything planned to the detail but somehow something might mess it up. And instead of thinking about what memories you could have made, focus on the ones which you are living right now.

Yours,

A fellow student

- Garnet

First Day into the Real World

I was a fresh flower just out of school,
Wanting to make a place in this world that is cruel.

An opportunity had knocked on my door while I was still learning;
My first thought had been, are my skills enough? Could I really start
earning?

Self - doubt and low self - esteem had been my friends since childhood,
Cowering me, even thought I was the brightest in the neighborhood. And
so, when I got the job, my happiness had been temporary, Dread filled
within me, blinding me of all that was merry.

I spent the next few days thinking of what would come next,
Would I enjoy my job or would I just tire myself for the monthly
paychecks?

Very soon the much awaited first day arrived;
I sat there and prayed to all the gods above, 'Please let me survive.'

In the very first minutes I was proved wrong;
By the end of lunch, I was singing the happy song.

Turns out everyone was in the same fear stricken boat,
And with everyone working as team we made sure it stayed afloat.

The new faces that I thought would terrify me,
Ended up making me feel like a warm day indoors, with blankets and a
cup of tea.

By the end of the day my pearl whites were out;
Not clattering in fear but smiling in the anticipation of how this experience
would pan out.

- Garnet

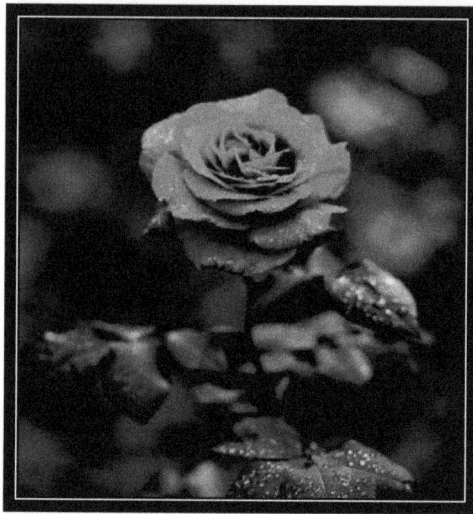

Pic credits: unsplash.com

R. Rose is a new writer for Bounce over Expectation. She held a Visual Arts Certificate and was born in Riverside, California, and raised in Hawaii. She enjoys: reading, writing, drawing, and spending time with family and loved ones.

You can find her at:
Instagram ID : @kpwrites808
Yourquote   : @kpwrites808
Medium   : @kprose

False Hope

When our relationship began, it felt like a dream,
I was oblivious to the warning signs.
Oblivious to the strange habits.
Oblivious to the feeling that something was wrong.

Indeed when you fall into love, it is blind.
You miss their faults.
You miss the meaning between the lines.
And you're open to manipulation.

From the beginning, it was all a lie.
Your love for me was a lie.
It wasn't until you were under the influence
That you told me the truth.

"I love you, but I'm not in love with you."
I held my growing baby as you spoke those words.
Tears ran down my face, my mother and your family
There to witness those unforgettable words.

Indeed, you never really loved your baby or me.
Yet, while you're here sober and working,
We're no longer together, and you act like you
Miss and love us.

I don't believe you.
No one does.
You say you want to be here for us,
But words from a fool are worth nothing.

I gave you one too many chances.
I will not allow you to hurt my daughter
And I again.
Your mind and heart are fickle.
I'm over you and your foolishness.

-Rose

My Shining Star

When you enter the world,
You shot out like a bullet.
You sweetly cried for comfort.
I called your name, and you calmed.

You already knew who I was.
This feeling was beyond what
I imagined and comprehended.
I was happier at that moment
than in any other moment of my life.

Honestly, you are my shining star.
My legacy, my somber responsibility,
That's filled with both sorrow, joy,
And growing pains.

We latched onto each other like glue,
Never to be separated.
God has used you to ground me.
You are the blessing I was waiting for
All my life.

I'm starting life all over.
Raising you is a pleasant yet sad experience.
I relive my childhood and the faults of my parents.

But because I know where they fall short,
I'll work more diligently to give you
A childhood I didn't have.

- Rose

Journey

Your hooves of thunder,
your tail of ancient freedom.
Your snort and whinny always
Accompanied a delightful dance.

Large almond eyes,
Dark-bay coat, black mane, and tail.
People abused you on and off the race track.
You were afraid of being saddled.

Your freedom, innocence, and trust,
Stripped from you.
Who were you to trust?
Why would you trust?

But still yet, when we met,
When I first rode you, despite my
Lack of knowledge.
You understood me.

We helped each other grow.
We helped each other trust again.
But I fell short and eventually neglected you.
I was too young and naive to realize what I had.

I wish I never sold you.
I wish I didn't give up.
I felt like you needed someone with more experience.
I wish I still had you.
I'm sorry for failing you, and I wish I could make it up to you.
I hope you're happier wherever you are.

-Rose

Working or Hardly Working

Working with people is a rollercoaster.
Some are sweet and understanding.
And others are impatient and rude.
Some employees are friendly and others not so much.

It's a part of life, and each of us has to experience it.
A drudgery 9-5 job feels aimless and torturous,
But if one finds or does a job that one enjoys
That turns into a different matter.

We each have a calling and a job to do.
What a wonderful thing when calling and duty
Collide into one's passion.
Life is no longer dreary but filled with purpose.

Each passion comes with a risk,
Are you willing to take that chance?
It's hard to get the ball rolling,
But once momentum hits, let it grow.

It took me a long while to let go and trust the process,
I'm still going back to the basics.
But as it is slowly growing, it seems to be worth it.
There's nothing to fear with God in control and leading the way.

Oh, how this process has taught me so much.
The process of learning never stops.
The process of growing never stops unless you allow it.
Never give up on your dreams
And never stop growing.

- Rose

Growing Pains

Life never stops moving forward,
So why do we sometimes stop?
Frozen in a moment of pain and loss,
Why do we build a home there?

Has life lost its meaning to you?
Have you forgotten that there is still another page to turn?
Life is but a moment with mini moments inside it.
Life's not to be comfortable all the time.

She beckons us to grow.
To grow, mature, and be complete:
Spiritually, financially, personally, and relationally.
Life is never dull, even in the mundane.

With my kiss with death,
I have learned that life only gets sweeter,
Especially after the trial.
It's hard work, but it's worth it.

Growing pains only last for a moment.
But the growth experienced is exponential.
Eighty to a hundred years is not enough
When lived in regret or constant learning.

Praise God for His hope for eternity,
With eternal life, eternal peace, and no suffering or death
Life will become the full experience it is supposed to be.
But for now, as we wait for His return,
We must learn vital lessons and grow our character.

– Rose

ANUSHREE CHAKRABORTY

She is Anushree chakraborty, pursuing BA in English Honours and is in her final year. She is an enthusiastic girl who loves to write, ink her feelings that she experiences. She was a department topper in her higher secondary. She loves travelling, visiting places, loves to hear people's stories. Her goal is to do something which will enrich our society and wants to make a better tomorrow.

Her quote is "Life is short, lets rock it together".

She will be contended if you appreciate her write ups and support her reach her goal to be a writer.

Unexpected Reality

ACCEPT YOUR REALITY WHICH IS OFTEN UNEXPECTED!

Why our expectations are uncertain and realities certain? This was my question when I was a teen.

As we age, our expectations changes. Being a toddler, crawling on the floor she expected to walk like others whom she saw daily and it did become a reality. In her pre-school years she expected to go to school and was admitted. I still remember her little desires of writing with pen as she was sick of using pencil. Little did she expect that her mistakes won't be erased anymore. And there she realised that her reality bounced over her expectation when she started inking down her life and couldn't erase the errors she caused as she aged. She became certain of her uncertainties. But the continuous celebration of her birthdays made her reach an age of being an adolescent. Her presumptions became unorthodox, offbeat and bizarre. She needed to look pretty, she wanted to be loved, be accepted and appreciated. But it didn't happen the way she wanted. People did criticise her, scorned her for not being beautiful and that 14-year-old girl regularly screeched on her mother's lap for not being accepted. Even in her dance class she was objectified for not being so and so and was body shamed. She was fettered. She couldn't concentrate on her studies, even got red mark in a subject. The ones whom she called her "Pals" mocked her for not securing a standard percentage.

One fine day she saw a physically handicapped man who didn't expect anyone to help him walk, instead worked hard himself to walk miles. That day she realised that the word "EXPECTATION" doesn't stands for everyone, every time.

She expected people to love her but never loved herself, expected from her teachers to give her good marks but never worked hard herself, expected everyone's loyalty.

A small example of our daily life is before we expect plants to give us oxygen,

---

We are expected to give carbon-dioxide in return.

(THE THING WE EXPECT FROM OTHERS, WE SHOULD BE THE ONE TO FULFILL IT FIRST.)

When a topper of your school or any educational degree tells you that she didn't work hard and has not even completed her syllabus, don't expect that she is telling the truth, rather be sure that she has completed her third revision. But she was a fool to expect that. But the day when she took her 11th grade result, her teacher told her, "you are a mediocre student. Your growth is very static. You neither improve nor deteriorate." She herself was surpassed listening this. Moreover, she didnt expect this. She came back home, opened her syllabus and what happened next was beyond her own expectation. A year later she topped her department. That day she learnt that why expectations are uncertain and realities certain and most importantly she learned what is EXPECTED REALITY.
She started accepting instead of expecting. Accepting her own identity, her own reality. She knew she can never erase her mistakes but these mistakes did make her a better individual. And then the world seemed distinctive for her. Because the moment she started loving herself, the world started loving her too. Her Expectations got Accepted because it was Expected of her by this Nature.

Expecting good marks was not in her hands, but preparation was. Expecting people to love her was not in her hands, but loving herself was. The word "EXPECTATION" should not be heaped scorn, because it depends on "whom to expect", "when to expect", and sometimes "why to expect" and if you have an answer, to this your expectations will be a reality.

- Anushree chakraborty

She is Expected!

She is expected to be Amy, docile, submissive.
She is expected to be dutiful, unquestioning, subservient, soft spoken,
sacrificing.
She is expected to fit in every role of being an "ideal daughter",
"someone's wife", "sacrificing mother", and is always considered to be
dependent on someone. Before marriage she is dependent on her "father"
and after marriage she is dependent on her "husband", aging she is
dependent on her "son".
She is expected to give birth to a "son". Even a "GIRL CHILD" is
considered as a burden in the family. The very moment the family comes
to know that it's a girl child, a would be mother is expected to kill her
child in the womb.
She is treated as if she is a drawing room embellishment. She is cursed for
her gender, treated inhumanly, even forced to brutal treatments since time
immemorial.
She was expected to accept a so-called tradition where the tradition itself
was burning them alive.
She is expected to love everybody but is never loved back.
She is not expected to visit her mother once in a while as her "in-laws"
house is considered her new home. Why is this sacrifice her own (only)?
She is strangled to death but is expected to be quiet because that is the
synonym for being a girl child.
She is expected to smile, not laugh.
She is expected to behave modestly, sit properly and many more.
She is expected to accept the societal norms even if that's suicidal.
She is expected to be inferior to men as we live in a patriarchal society,
where marrying a guy even now most of the girls gets their title changed, a
child born gets the title of his father. Where's the role of a mother? Oh!
She is expected to be in kitchen.
Amidst these expectations of others, she burned her own.
Are her expectations still valid?
Can't she be accepted?

THEY WILL ASK YOU TO BEHAVE LIKE "WOMEN" YOU WILL
SHOW THEM WHO A "REAL WOMAN" IS!

WHY IS SHE ALWAYS EXPECTED AND NEVER ACCEPTED!
WHY?

If a man is expected to earn his living,
A woman will help her by earning her own living.
If a woman can cook, a man can too.
After all its all about balancing each other,

JUST TO BE WITH AND RESPECT ONE ANOTHER!

- Anushree chakraborty

APARNA SINGH

Aparna Singh is a budding writer at spectrum of thoughts for 'Bounce over Expectation'. She spends a lot of her time reading. She mainly pens poetry to feed the creative inclinations within. A lover of cookies and naps. She isn't trained into writing, only a novice with the propensity to put feelings to paper. She is definitely interested into chitter-chattering about books

You can find her at-
Instagram ID : @aparnaherondale
Poetic handle : @poetic_spice

I Hope You Understand

Every morning when the Ra-god streams in through the little spaces in the
curtains,
Her warm smile rises from her plump lips to her iridescent eyes,
Rising to strong, interlaced, trustworthy fingers; it's everyone's chimera,
is it not?
She sings to her fluttery heart
'Shh- I hope you understand'

Sitting on the shiny bonnet of his vintage Chevrolet Corvette,
To walking down the aisle in a long forgotten dress

A 'match made in heaven' they said,
A 'journey full of joy' they pronounced

Shimmering liquids they sizzled,
& crooned in glee,
'I hope you understand'

No one could've fathomed; when the sickening began
Tragedy has soft footsteps they say,
The walls and tapestries shivered in disgust,
Helplessly proclaimed-
'I hope you understand'

The inconsolable shrieks, the sweat-laden foreheads; duvets hide,
The masked fears that lay concealed under the shut eyes,
A promise that the chapped lips make to the chattering teeth,
'I hope you understand'

Being chained by the societal norms
Each day she threw her rights in the deathly pit of deforms
To her broken fingers and her age old whip marks; she reassured,
Thrashed and forlorn,
'I hope you understand'

- Aparna Singh

The Lost Autumn

The crack of the dawn brings
In the light,
But will it decide;
What my future will look like?

       The "adopted child syndrome"
       I have given it a thought;
       Not just today; but forever since

All things gaudy;
Have a tinge of dark in it
All things shimmery;
Lack a 'spark' within.

       Permanence, Stability,
       'Words' my short existence
       Has seldom been acquainted with

Autumn has a voice of its own,
Tis' the intricacy & meaning;
That she has shown

       But her carpets are;
       Often crushed
       Her love misguided & misjudged

I saw 'em the day before,
The woman with the kind eyes,
The man with milky smiles

       Am I to be theirs?
       Who is to decide?

Will they leave me on the lost path,
Again?
Do I deserve them?
Is it finally my time?

Ten years hence,
The choice I made;
Its been the most marvellous ride,
Each morning; I wake up
To hugs and pats,
Each night;
An array of bedtime stories
Full of eclat

The lost autumn;
Yes, she has been found,
A princess in herself;
But without the sparkling crown

Dreams;
that clung to the cotton of her pillow,
Soon became her wings to fly.

Yes, it took courage
But fate soon revealed its form,
Yes, that is what had changed it all.

- Aparna Singh

SAISHA JAIN

An aspiring writer who strives to learn and bring her thoughts down on paper. Saisha Jain is a 14-year-old student of Springdales School, Dhaula Kuan. She loves to spend time reading books, going through bookstores and make edits.

Quote : 'When messages stop being only words but rather a connection of their own, they become what you imagine—those binding graphic words.'

Instagram ID   : @magicmusings_
Wattpad   : @sj162001
Mail ID   : saishajain16@gmail.com /
                                    16sj2001@gmail.com

Set in Stone

Expectations that run through blood, skin, and bone,
Our minds screech to leave them alone.
Hearts open to the voices screaming,
The yearning desire—one day shall come true and gleaming.
Yet the mind remains at battle with itself.
Crying, wailing, the shouting and yelling, deafen ourselves.
Try as we might, think of expectations as a blight,
They don't go down without a fight.
Try and try till we tire to the bone,
It is a skill we cannot hone.
Those expectations set in stone,
Better to just leave them alone.

Hope and expectations,
Lead to believe as manifestations.
Not all comes true,
Often lies and lies pile up.
Unable to remove as if stuck by glue,
Lounging together in our minds' club.
Simple for us to believe it all,
Lies which pull us by their enticing call.
Heart-breaking expectations set in stone,
Better to leave them alone.
When knowing that in pain you will groan,
Just leave them alone!
Expectations always set in stone,
Let down we are, reality never being its clone.

- Saisha Jain

The Search

Believe we do, in having a purpose to complete
And chase after it, till we tire our feet.
Like heroes and kings
An' all their glorious reign,
But in the end, all is in vain.

And when what we seek is what we find,
We are too blind, to see with the mind.
We never know when we drink the numbing wine;
'Tis is with what we dine,
And search for purpose given by divine.

Fools we are, to not see our chance.
For it is up to us, to water the flower.
Fame and glory, of it we dream
And at our hopefulness,
Amused, the sun shall beam.

The same as all I did,
Of going on adventures
After the goodbye I bid.
But stuck I was in stories
That was the answer to my pleas.

But excitement and thrill and danger felt,
So thus, given was the home in which I now dwelt.
Perhaps it was my expectations, high indeed,
But I learnt to dream of the reality within my reach.

-Saisha Jain

Remains of Reality

Sweater than honey it may seem,
Reality, bitter than ever imagined.
Rain of happiness we suppose it showers,
Floods of sorrow accompany its arrival.

It can be your beautiful Spring
It can be sad Autumn compared to expectations,
Poisoning the heart held by a hopeful string.
Beware! The sea of reality a dangerous one,
Great and mighty the tides are to overcome.

You can either drown, or you can survive,
But you don't always get for what you strive.
May be astounding
Often gets the heart pounding,
This life which we lead spiralling.

Expectations of magic,
Of adventure and wonder.
Everlasting fire,
Or warnings by thunder.

Yet remain ashes,
The embers flickering.
Suddenly sad it may seem,
And not so endearing.

All we wish, then becomes faulty.
Reminded by the brutality,
The flickering remains of reality.

-Saisha Jain

Frustrated On Expectations Or Reality?

December 21, 2021
Tuesday

Dear Diary,

It has been a long time, hasn't it? But I suppose we can't exactly call ourselves acquaintances now, can we? I mean two entries and then gone. It isn't exactly my fault you know. I started a journal during the lockdown, what was I thinking? I expected to have things to right—how my day went, how I felt.

I mean, I'm no Emerson, but I expected to have at least something to write about! Stories are way more adventurous than life. Now all I do—all I can do—is attend my classes, do my work…and think and think—and get lost in my thoughts. It's funny, isn't it? How I expected life to be so much more. More adventures, more stories, more excitement. And now—the most happening thing that is taking place is that my exams are coming, and I must study.

There are times our hopes are so high that our reality becomes a nightmare. Others, the results make our hearts leap. It doesn't matter what we hoped— the universe isn't here to fulfil our expectations; we must accept what reality offers to us. We all look forward to the time when our expectations may come true, but if it does so every time, there is nothing to be anticipated for. It's our reality that makes us wish and if expectations came true, it wouldn't be reality. Expectations and reality co-exist and without being let down, we can't get up.

Saisha

-Saisha Jain

Leap of Faith

Dear Reader,

Can we talk about Santa? Because I know that is one experience in which all our expectations came crumbling down. I mean, who hasn't tried staying awake, only to find there is no chubby man in a red suit with a big and fluffy beard? No? Okay.

I don't remember many stories where the results of reality were totally different than my expectations (except maybe my memory. I didn't expect that to be that of a 90-year-old's). We all expect things, wishes which don't come true. Like I dreamt that my grandmother would be there when I publish my first work, or how I expected my parents to give me a bigger bookshelf because they know me. Like, a small bookshelf with about 25 books is just not enough! How could this be sufficient for the other books I'm going to buy!?

Why I'm writing such an informal letter is because if I do otherwise it will be another lecture from your principal—which just puts a lot of pressure on you. Know what that means? Expectations. It's just another word for it. 'Worrying means you'll suffer twice,' they say. I say that expecting means you'll cry twice, even if it is due to different emotions.

Anyways, like every young girl, I've dreamt of being an artist, a dancer, singer, you name it. When I officially started writing and told my mom what I wanted to do, it was great! Now? I have four books, each have at-least two chapters—that's it. People come asking, done with your book? And all I want to do is laugh hysterically, and then sigh—nope. My goal to finish one book by the end of the year went down the drain and I wanted to scream because I had no idea what I was doing. I'm sure my work was flowing down the sewer my neighbour might be walking across now. Then one day, I completed the plot of my story and got to be a part of this book! What I mean is, expectations don't always have to be higher than what we get. Sometimes, we downgrade ourselves and get a reality better than estimated. Sometimes, it's not about what you envisage—it's about taking a leap of faith.

Yours truly,
Saisha.

-Saisha Jain

RUPWANTI KANU

Rupwanti Kanu is a budding writer at Spectrum Of Thoughts for ' Bounce over expectation'. She is appearing intermediate in CBSE. She hails from 'Deoria'. She enjoys pursuing write their own views, singing, painting and sports' during the free hours.

A World Full Of Happiness

If there was a city of happiness, there would be no sorrow,

If there was a world beyond this world, it would not be so evil today,

If there was a fairyland, helping everyone with magical committees,

If there was an invisible place, it would be invisible to all the negativity,

If there was power in hand, there would be solutions to all troubles,

I wish there was a world full of happiness, where there was happiness and peace for everyone,

I wish there was a world full of happiness where there was happiness lies in the atmosphere.

- Rupwanti Kanu

City Of Fantasy

A city made of imagination,
The city of my mind where all the times fantasies,
Imagining more, write more and discussing everything with own,

There is magic in every word that compels one to imagine,
The ocean of imagination is so vast that it never fills up and never dries up,
Some fantasizing is the work of fantasies,

Fantasies never come true but sometimes our fantasies turn into reality,
The lack of control of my mind on itself is the identity of being in the city of fantasies,

Imagination is the melody that comes out of my heart,
Which removes every difficulty and becomes a home through word,
Every time comforts the mind by reducing my unfathomable pain,

Imagination become with me in every moment because of just I am over thinking about anything,
Just listen to me and write down some of my imagination and views with a pen on a piece of paper,

There is only one city that resides inside my heart,
A city of fantasies.

- Rupwanti Kanu

In The Sky

In the sky,
If I am a star, I can shine like nobody shine,
In the sky,
If I am a cloud, I can help all the needy,
In the sky,
If I am a galaxy, I can hide all my pain in the huge galaxy,
In the sky,
If I am a sun, I can burn all the negativity,
In the sky,
If I am an aeroplane I can fly above the high,
In the sky,
If I am a wind, I can blew all over the universe
In the sky,
If I am a Bird, I can flying like nobody flies,
In the sky,
If I have a power, I can spread positivity all over the world.

- Rupwanti Kanu

Bounce Over Expectation

Once upon a time, when I was so sick. I had lost all my hope. I thought I could never be better. I felt that I was taking my last breath.

It was raining one night and it was raining all night. It was a stormy night. I was all alone at home that night. Everyone went out that night no one was there. With the broken hut the raindrops were soaking my dry courtyard.

Sometimes my breathing was too fast and sometimes too slow. I was not normal. My little Hut looked like it would fall and that day I felt that I would say goodbye to this world. That day tears float in my darken eyes, but I didn't have the strength to even wipe off my tears.

My weeping eyes stopped at a moment on a little bird who was saving her nest and her children too by getting wet in the rain. At that time a ray of hope arose in my heart. May I start thinking beyond my negative thoughts that how can I protect my hut from heavy rain.

I don't know where this thought came that I have to get up to save my hut. May I come back from the door of my death with positive vibes. A new hope arose in me, a new way was found. That day I changed my mind as well as my thoughts about life.

That day I learned the right way to live life. That day my heart realized that there is a world beyond this imagination. Life is the book which tells to fight with difficulties and not to run away from them. That day with this lesson I stood up again to save my little broken hut as well as my own life which I was easily losing.

It is true that God has no form, no shape and no religion. He had to teach me something good even in my despair. Our expectations are not always true, sometimes something bigger becomes bigger than our expectations. Sometimes our expectations bounce over our life.

- Rupwanti Kanu

खुद को जान के तो देखो

दर्द दिल की गहराई से पूछो,
उससे पहले दिल में उतर के तो देखो,
मिल रहा है कितना सुकून इस बेदर्द जुंबा से तो पूछो,
कड़वे मेरे बोल, साफ है मगर दिल,
एक बार इस दिल की धड़कन तो सुन के देखो,
रहेगा न एहसास तुम्हें खुद का,
एक बार अपने दिल को इस दिल से जोड़ के तो देखो,

मुझे किसी से कोई उम्मीद नहीं,
तुम एक बार खुद से खुद को प्यार कर के तो देखो,
मिल रही हैं राहतें इस बिखरे दिल को समेटने में,
मुश्किल तो बहुत है रास्ते,
मगर जीने का जज़्बा ला के तो देखो,

सुकून तो कहीं नहीं है,
एक बार खुद से खुद को वक्त दे के तो देखो,
शीशे की तरह, कांटों से भरा रास्ता है,
एक बार इस आग में जल के तो देखो,
फूल की खुशबू, ख्वाबों के रंग,
है छड़ भर का पल जीवन में ग़म,
एक बार अपने भीतर एक छोटी सी आश जगा के तो देखो,
कठीन है इस बेमतलब संसार में जीना,
एक बार खुद को पहचान के तो देखो।।

- Rupwanti Kanu

SAI KUMAR CHALLA

Sai Kumar Challa is an Embedded Engineer. He is from Narsapuram, Godavari Dist, Andhra Pradesh. He enjoys living in nature so he started his own you tube channel and describes the nature in his way. He loves playing and watching cricket.

Instagram ID : @saikumarchalla9
You Tube   : Saikumarchalla9
Email Id   : Saikumarchalla9999@gmail.com

Middle Class Life -
Struggles and Overcomes

A boy name called Sai who was from a middle class family, his father was a daily wager and a sole person to earn income. But he made sure to provide education to his children, though his neighbours taunted and demotivated him saying he is wasting his money on children education instead of sending them for the work. He never listened to those words and encouraged his children (Sai,Satya and Jyothi) to reach their positions. And coming to Sai's mother, she is a homemaker. She supports her husband and children with their decision and never expects any wishes (gold and saree's etc..).

As Sai is the youngest of all those three who is more active in all the works. Sai studied at local government school and got very good marks in all the academics, by seeing that neighbours chanted and de motivated though he got a good marks but he will never get a job .Sai took it as a challenge to get a job as against to their expectation, As said actions speak a lot than words .

Reaching to the goals and expectations takes lot of hardwork, struggle and downfalls to meet the reality. As a first step of the challenge he has to leave his hometown, family and friends and go to another city to complete his studies. As this was the first time to him that leaving his family. So, he was unable to concentrate on his studies. He lost the track which leaded him to lose of campus placements. This made him realize the taunts of his neighbours and he became sad and felt alone. Even though their family members never forced him to get a campus placements and he returned to his hometown after completing his studies.

Few days passed in the sadness and he was engrossed in his household works. His brother, Satya understood his feelings and motivated him again; One fine day, he recollected his challenge. He understood, if he sits like that he can't achieve the goal and started applying for jobs again and again. His family and friends encouraged and motivated him a lot.

During the phase, one of his friends suggested him that to take a course which was related to his interest and help him in getting the job, which excited him. He quickly applied for the training course and after all attempts, He got selected for the position to take training. Now this was the crucial time to him to get a job and he worked hard for 6 months, continuously without any distractions and expectations to reach the goal and prove his talent to everyone.

Finally, his hardwork paid off, he got selected in one of his dream job and he conquered his challenge which he has taken during his childhood. In parallel his brother, Satya also got the job as software engineer.

Sai joined into his desired company as a fresher. He struggled a lot and he studied and learnt many things from his colleagues, who became friends in a short span of time to understand and keep up with the role which helped him to handle things on his own. This was the life changing moment to their family and both, Sai and Satya shut their neighbours' mouth.

Life is full of surprises but we have to work hard equivalently to unlock and get the rewards.

- Sai Kumar

Journey to the YouTube

Kumar lives in a place which has many scenic beauties of colourful nature. He used to watch many videos about other places outside the country and used to get fascinated with the scenarios. One day, he got an idea to show his hometown beauties to the world through YouTube and he started a channel which is **saikumarchalla9** and he started to explore many unseen places in his hometown which going on became his passion.

When he started his channel he didn't expect the people will watch his videos but he was shocked when his videos went viral which helped to get motivated, upload more videos and explore many places.

Sometimes we won't expect the things but it is planned more than our expectations, this is the reality of life. We generally plan for shorter joy but in reality God has planned a longer joy and permanent happiness.

- Sai Kumar

RAMYA DEEPTHI

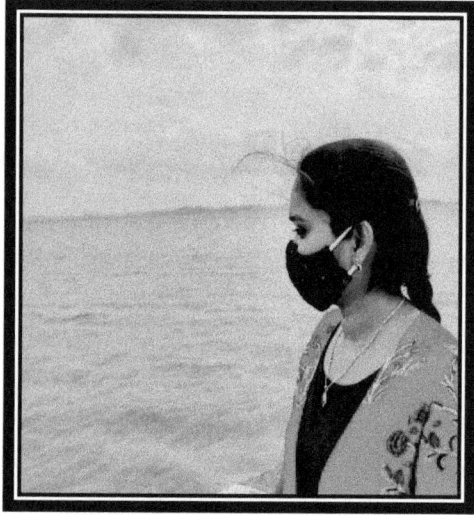

Ramya deepthi is an aspiring content writer, who is also an IT engineer by profession. In her perspective, writing lets you to express your inner feelings without speaking directly to anyone. So who is an introvert like her can try to express their feelings in the forms of words on a paper.

Bounce Over Expectations

Expectation is a word that almost gets connected in each and every individual's life...

The word seems to be simple but it meant to be soo much that the one individual gets happier with its final outcome or he can be suppressed into the utmost pressure and pain which he cannot imagine when he thought of it at first glimpse.....

This word will not leave any aspect of that individual whether it might be his emotions...relations...education...financial

status...job...happiness...love...what not anything and everthing..it has its own essence on each one of this which leads to the destruction or evolution of that individual....

And we besides men/ women would make this word as part of our lives and without this our lives are not adventurous anymore...

From the very seconds our life comes into existence ie., you are in your mammas womb this word expectation has its own charge on your life....Like your parents expect that you would be particularly girl/boy...and then at your child stage they expect you to be extraordinarily good at studies/ anything...and then when you are graduated they expect you to be in a good paying job and then expect you to have a good wife and then for grand children again...

This cycle goes on and on and on....this is just in your parents perspective but there are many people around you...with you who have their own sort of expectations on you....and you yourself put expectations on your life to be that or this....also you'll have expectations on the people around you....

This is it...it's life and a never ending process

In this one process of individuals life he goes through many ups and downs but these hurdles he experience are only for one final moto i.e., SATISFACTION which brings him happiness

but he never realises that this satisfaction will vanish for the very next minute as that one word dominates over it... which is EXPECTATION to have more, more and more than what we have...And there he looses his own happiness, peace and thrives for more and more and moreee...

So learn to have peace of SATISFYING over things you have...which makes you to enjoy the true essence of life....

- Ramya Deepthi

JAYA BHARATHI GOVINDARAJU

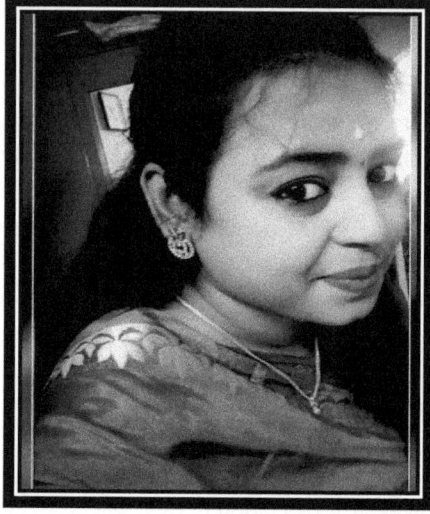

Jaya Bharathi Govindaraju is a poet / writer at "Spectrum Of Thoughts" for an Anthology named "Bounce Over Expectations". She is an English Post-Graduate. An English Teacher, by profession and a passionate writer in the language of English and Tamil. She takes "J.B" as her pen name to all her literary works.

She strongly believes that "Greatness of being born lies with the language shared and communicated" .

You can find and enjoy her writings at
Instagram ID   : @jai bharrati
Your quotes pen name : J.B (jaibharrati)
Mail ID   : ayrus.sai@gmail.com

To be Successful in Life, Bounce over Your Expectations

Like all other girls I too dreamt of a fairy-tale marital life,
Like every other girl I was also tagged as a goodwife,
With plenty of voices, and many number of oaths to promises.
I was solemnly knotted for life, by just walking around the fire seven
customary times.
I was Nostalgic that everything happened precisely to adorn my awaited
highlife!

Oh! Months marched, years parched with most of my days grey and pale.
Yet, nothing to cajole me for the things I dreamt with a great morale.
I tried adapting and fixing myself into this life, with every chance of mine.
I failed and wailed to everyone I knew, blindly hoping to repair my maze
life in twine.
I moved away from people I liked and turned so fragile like the sediment
shale.

- Jaya Bharathi

Little Things Matter

Little things matter, yet greater things ruin our lives,
Over all the differences and unexpected illusions, my poor heart thrives.
Adding to my desires, dreams and expectations I was blessed to be a
mother. Nevertheless I found everything I trusted to be bogus, and sadly
nothing to bother. I gave birth to a new Life, a contemporary phase that
greatly arrives.

I never tried to disguise myself in rife .
It was just a matter of trying a bit harder to attain my ever dreamt fairy-
tale Life,
All went upside down, and I was finally portrayed as a Clown,
I chose to cry like a baby without mom, left withered and meant only to
mourn,
I bounced over my expectations and here I am, with a real tale for Life.

Praise the little things you come across.
Smile and cry before you lose your toss.
Life has all that you need, and not all that you greed.
Look around with a magnifier, choose to chase happiness at full speed.
Keep moving with the rhythm of life, and never take a pause.

Take Life with all heart and move on with a new start,
Spread love, knowledge and positivity before you actually depart.
Every minute is a chance to revive and relive.
Every relationship and struggle is a blessing to survive
Bounce over your expectations! Our life is an authentic tale, never retreat
or regret.

"This poem is an attempt to express how every woman bounces over their
expectations in personal and social Life . Beyond all those expectations,
how each woman shines and paves their path of strong Identity, though
she is undefined, unnoticed and least appreciated. May be each woman
can relate to these words and feel proud of their whole journey in these 30
lines . It is a strong statement that - Every individual can overcome their
regrets upon one's own life and on the go motivate themselves to be more
progressive and successful by accepting or forgiving their expectations

" The poem obeys "Quintain form" or "limerick poetic form" with 6 stanzas, 5 lines each stanza having the Rhyme Scheme : AABBA.

- *Jaya Bharathi*

Vocabulary

Parched: dried out with heat

Grey: without interest or character, dull .

Goodwife: the female head of a household.

Highlife: an extravagant social life as enjoyed by wealth

Morale: confidence, enthusiasm and discipline of a person at a particular time.

Cajole: persuade someone or to do something by sustained coaxing.

Mazed: confused or puzzled.

Twine: several things joined together

Shale: sedimented hard clay rock which is easily breakable

Bogus: not genuine or true

Rife: wide spread, a undesirable, unpleasant happening

Mourn: feeling sad and regretful

Relive: live through again in one's imagination or memory

Revive: restore to life or getting back to normal

Authentic: genuine and not a copy of something

Regret: feeling sad and disappointed over something

- Jaya Bharathi

DEVESHWAR THAKUR

Devesh grew up in the mighty mountains of Chamba, Himachal Pradesh. He is an engineering professional and enjoys writing, singing, and playing guitar during his free hours. He is a photography enthusiast too and entered in top 33% best photographers in **35AWARDS** thematic contest.

You can find him at:
Instagram ID : deveshpixels
               pure_n_peace
Your Quote   ; dquoteinfinite

The Dilemma

The sound of rain drops seeping through our roof into the pan kept beside me, I remember.

I remember the touch of the sprinkled drop after striking the collected water in the pan.

The aroma of clay plastered on the walls when they got wet during rain, I remember.

I remember the warmth of fire burning in the clay oven during winter.

I remember the taste of ash on the wheat bread cooked in the clay oven.

The feeling of snow walks after the season's first snowfall.

I still remember that sweet pain on my fingertips when I warmed them on fire after the snow fun.

I always live that moment when my father made us the very first dice and played with us during the winters.

I will never forget those winters echoed with music from my father, which inspired us throughout our childhood.

I write, sing, and play; all of these creative traits were passed down from my mother and father.

We grew up like the Prince and the Princess.

It was like a fine picture playing in front of an applauded audience, but no one knew what was happening backstage.

We had nothing but happiness.

Now the scent of flowers has faded, the lush green grass has evanesced into the ground.

People say time is powerful, but it is the irony of life.

Life passes away in the dynamics of existence and purpose.

We must explore the entirety of life and live each moment as if it were our last.

- Deveshwar Thakur

Purpose of Life

Shiven, an aspiring advertising agency professional working for a new start up in Mumbai, wakes up early at 5:30 a.m. with a routine of cardio exercises followed by a cup of tea and later a light breakfast with soothing music at his rented oneBHK flat located in Navi Mumbai, since Navi Mumbai is comparatively cheaper than Mumbai. So, he had to catch the local train at 6:54 a.m. from Navi Mumbai to Nariman Point, where his office was located.

He used to light a cigarette and buy a Parle-G biscuit for the stray dog who was always waiting for him to feed him five minutes before arriving at work.

His boss, K.Bhaskaran, an ugly fat ass, always keeps an eye on his subordinates for their arrival.

Shiven never missed a day to see the name plate outside his boss's cabin, K.Bhaskaran, Creative Director. He has deep aspirations to climb every ladder in his career. Shiven was working hard on a project for months, and many times the security guy named Vishnu came up and reminded him to leave.

The very next day, Bhaskaran told; Shiven, it is a big day today for all of us to get a 100 crores advertising deal with prestigious Delta Formations, if everything goes as planned.

Unfortunately, things did not go as planned, and the company lost the deal.

Bhaskaran was mad at Shiven since it was his chance to earn a fortune promotion.

Shiven did not say anything to Bhaskaran and left the office in a deep void.It takes him two hours to return home by local train from Mumbai.

While travelling back home, Shiven had a feeling of failure and was thinking about all the arduous work that had not paid off.

Suddenly, he was overwhelmed by the compelling aura around him. Shiven gazed up, a sage in saffron coloured attire with Rudraksha neckpieces behind the long beard almost hiding his neck, a Vermillion Tilak on the forehead with three horizontal lines called Tripundra on his arms as well, and most prominently, long, unkempt tresses pulled up right on the head in a circular motion, was sitting just in front of him.

Shiven expressed with his inquisitive eyes and asked the Sage, "What is the purpose of life?"

Sage: What do you understand by life?

Shiven: Life, in my opinion, is full of challenges that we face, fail, and conquer, but today I feel as if these beliefs have no meaning for me.

Sage: You are born to live life, not to think about and invent all kinds of purposes for it. Life does not need any purpose. If you experience this life in its fullness, life is a purpose unto itself.

The station arrived, and Shiven stepped out of the train in a rush, along with the crowd. He turned back to Sage, but he could not see him again.

It was 9:45 p.m. when he reached home. He made an omelette of two eggs and served them with two brown breads for dinner. Shiven was in deep delusion about his conversation with the Sage. His unconscious mind was retrieving all those aspirations he planted, but the conscious mind had beliefs about what the Sage told him.

He closed his eyes and the sage within him appeared and said, "I am not what you believe. I am you, and you are everything that you see around you. "What you have gained and what you have lost are similar. Desire creates greed, greed creates hatred, and hatred brings delusion, so why is this agony buried deep inside? Living in the fullness of life without any purpose is reality.

"It's our mind that creates a society of love and hate, good and bad; society makes it real."

- Deveshwar Thakur

The Awakening

I could feel the cold mist in the freezing wind. I could hear the whistling of the wind in my ears like a peaceful piece of music.

It was white everywhere; the snow had never shone like a diamond before.

I was half way to reaching the top of the mountain when suddenly the snow storm started blowing so heavily that I was not able to see farther.

There was no shelter to stay for a while, and my breath was calling for a living.

I fell down on the ground and tried breathing heavily. With blurred vision, all I could see was a saffron colour at a distance.

Shiven! Shiven! A voice echoed with interrupted bangs.

Suddenly, I woke up and swirled my eyes around. I felt like someone was knocking on my door and shouting my name.

It was 9:30 am. I got up in half-sleep and opened the door, but no one was out there.

Suddenly, I came back to my senses. Oh, no! Bhaskaranis going to kill me; Shiven murmured in anxiety.

He rushed to the washroom and got dressed in just five minutes.

At 9:30 am, he caught the local train to the office and arrived in a hurry.

There was a deep silence at the workplace.

Vishnu, what's the matter? Shiven asked. Whyis everyone in a deep void?

Vishnu said: Sahab, Bhaskaran Sahab encountered cardiac arrest at about 9:15 am this morning. Holy shit! Where is he now? Shiven asked with a deep concern.

He was rushed to the nearby hospital in an office ambulance, Vishnu said.

Shiven picked up his phone and thought about making a call to Bhaskaran, but he dropped it. Then he reached for his desk and a message popped up on his system.

A recall for the "Final Presentation on Modern Advertising" on Teams at 11:30 am.

Shiven: What the hell? It's a recall presentation for our last 100 crore lost deal.

Shiven talked to himself and said, "Shiven, it's your final chance to prove yourself." But without Bhaskaran, how am I going to pitch it?

Shiven's legs were tumbling and his heart was beating fast. He closed his eyes and remembered Sage's word, "*You are born to live life, not to think about and invent all kinds of purposes for life. Life does not need any*

purpose. If you experience this life in its fullness, life is a purpose unto itself.
"

Shiven opened his eyes and everything was like the wheel of time had stopped and he had stepped into another world. There was no greed for success, no fear of losing, and no future thoughts. Everything was crystal clear.

At 12:30 pm, he finished his presentation on behalf of Bhaskaran.

This time, Shiven was not very excited about what he was going to achieve or lose. But had a clear thought of "I did my best."

Suddenly, a call was received from the hospital that we had lost Bhaskaran. That was the moment when I realised that life is nothing but a pre-programmed system. When the purpose is over, the programme is uninstalled and a new version is uploaded.

At 04:15 pm, a message popped up:

"Congrats team!!

We are honoured to work together and make our brand grow in heaven and hell.

Roger Nick, CEO,Delta formations.

A loud bang jolts him out of his slumber.

Holy shit! Was it a dream? Shiven took a deep breath and smiled.

The window behind him was banging on the wall with the wind.

It was raining heavily and showed signs of a hurricane.

Shiven closed the window and got back into his bed.

 "What we see is a reflection of our mental manifestation of what we wanted to see."

- Deveshwar Thakur

PUNEET VERMA

PUNEET VERMA just likes to write about what he experienced and observed, have been through many phases of life and still in the process of learning.

Instagram ID : @words_world_007
Email ID   : puneetverma6696@gmail.com
Your Quote   : https://www.yourquote.in/puneet-verma-btt3c/quotes
LinkedIn ID : https://www.linkedin.com/in/puneet-verma-16a9a1199

A Letter to My Younger Self

This letter is to my younger self. when I felt that everything is possible everything is magical I was living in a place where all the rules were decided by me, but everything seems unrealistic when I grow up something I want to teach my younger self, that I wish I was aware of it know when I was younger.

Hobbies

I know today I like to play the guitar, I like to play table tennis, badminton but when I grow up this is not possible for you to arrange your time for your hobbies especially if you are not able to make a career out of it or get any monetary benefit but it important for your mental growth these are helpful to calm your nerves.

Of course, your primary goal in future will be your career but just arrange your time for 2 hours on a working day or even more and big lots on weekends but don't try to avoid your it, hobbies are important because it will make you aware of your existence otherwise seen many people keep on working day and night.

Hobbies will be like meditation for you which will be helpful when you do the process which is required for your career goal. Just try to be as good in your hobby as you can not in comparison to someone else.

These hobbies will be your best friend when you are in the face of adversity or the face of failure.

Friends

Do you know the simplest way to change yourself is by Changing your company, friends have a major impact on you because if you be with them most of the time and also connect with them they can change your entire personality and also as it said that "a man is known by his company".

Choose your friends wisely, your friend should be the person you want to become in your life. Sometimes your parents are not able to understand you but your friends are with whom you can share anything and they connect with you immediately.

Your real friends are those with whom you don't need to use any filter they are ok with what you are and it can also be an opposite gender you just need to maintain the line which the other gender has created.
But the reality is your friend may not always be in touch with you and it is completely ok because they also want to move on in life they will also meet different people, they will make new friends and you will also do the same but one thing that will remain the same is your bond with them whenever you meet your friends the bond will remain the same.

But always remember one thing the bad company is better than being alone.

Parents
I know that at this age you love your parents or sometimes hate them when they shout at you but at this age, you don't know the importance of being with you.
You may think that you have many friends who are there for you when you need them, they will help you selflessly but the reality is that there are very few friends of yours who love you or help you selflessly may be one or two but parents will always love or help you selflessly.
Parents will never be in their dreams think anything wrong for you. Just try to share your feelings with them about what you feel for them because you don't know how much they will live, just try to communicate your love until it became too late. They just need your quality time with you so don't use any gadgets when you are with them. And sometimes your thoughts may not match with them and there is nothing wrong with it always ready to listen to their point of view also, because they are more experienced than you and also they will never think anything wrong for you considering this reason made your decision.

They will always remain a visible God for you.

Failures
Failure is the most important thing in life, you will not be able to learn from your success as much you learn from your failures. They are the best teacher in the world.

The problem is no one in your family, friends or society will teach you how to deal with failures they always tell you that you should win but sometimes it's ok to fail and if you learn from your failures then failing is worth it in your life.
When you face failures you start realising that you have more patients, decision-making skills and more power to endure pain. When you fail you start realising the importance of your parents and you get to know who is

your real friends are, friends are not who is with you with your success real friends stand with you when you really need them.

When you are in the phase of failure always maintain that mindset that this failure will help you in future, these failures are preparing you for your future battle you may not understand today but one day you will understand it when you connect your past failures with present strengths. And one shahrukh khan said in his ted talk " it's not the absence of failure that will make you successful, it's your response to failure that actually helps to buffer the reverses that you experience, so do fail and it's ok to fail sometimes.

It doesn't matter how big or small your failure is what matter is what next step you will take after being failed.

Give Some Time To Yourself

In whatever phase of life you are just given some time to yourself, just take a pause and enjoy being yourself.

It is very important because if you be alone for some time you will be able to see what's going on in your life from being away from it.

It will also help you to get some insights that are not possible if you always busy with your work. It will be like a meditation for you, just walk in the park, walk on your terrace and just make your mind calm and enjoy the openness around you.

Sometimes you may feel stuck, bored in this situation just take a pause and see yourself as a third person and analyse your situation and talk to yourself about what the next step is required otherwise you keep ongoing with a flow, you should always lead your life.

At last, I just want to say life is much more than this success or failure do what you love doing and if you are not able to get monetary benefit out of it then don't leave it just nurture it like a hobby.

- Puneet Verma

Facing the Unexpected Failures

Date - 25/01/2020

Today is my birthday on this day I used to enjoy my entire day be it giving a party to my friends celebrate it with my parents, relatives and neighbours. I used to wait for this day for an entire year I always try to make this day better than my previous birthdays.

I used to believe that my life will always be smooth I will be the most successful person but the reality is different. I used to enjoy my birthdays when I was in school or when I have just started pursuing my chartered accountancy course. On this birthday I will become 22 years old and still in the second level (CA-intermediate) of a chartered accountancy course (for your information there are three stages of this course namely foundation, intermediate, final before giving finals we have to do 3 years of articleship under a chartered accountancy firm)

One of my cousin brothers was made fun of me because I am 22 years old and still only a BCom graduate because at the same age he was a BTech graduate and started his job. which is the worst thing a person can do by making fun of someone's lowest level and he was also not graduated from a good college it was just a below-average college.
It is not like I am poor in academics it happened because of a lack of guidance and overconfidence at the early stage of my course. So after all the celebrations of my birthday, I talk with my parents and they give me the validation and blessings that I have a strong academic background I shouldn't have to feel hurt because of the words of other people or because of my bad failing experience. But I didn't sleep a full night by thinking about it continuously.

Date - 27/01/2020

Today have seen so many videos on YouTube of those people that were in the same stage where I am today and talk with 4 people who are already chartered accountants, 3 of them were in the same place where I am today means they are the right person to take guidance from.

At last, I drop to the conclusion that being practical I will give just the last chance to myself and after that, I will move towards other courses which are very important because this will create urgency in my mind and will be good for my long term career also.

It is very difficult for me to accept that me being always in the top 5 at the school level is facing such difficulty in these exams, but the hard reality is I am facing it although learning at every step.

I have decided that this time I will give my 200% on this process and every day I will achieve my day targets. Before my exam, I will not think about any plan B. I have made a proper plan on a piece of paper, and have written my strength and weaknesses. I have also written my target marks to achieve. I have made a concrete plan now only two things I have to do is execute it and perform in my exams.

This time I am well prepared BUT one thing more without which I cannot perform is to fire the belief system in me for that I read think and grow rich and many more videos available on youtube.

I stay away from negative people and increase my concentration by meditation. This time I am starting afresh with trying to be fit mentally and physically as much as possible which is after failing quite difficult for me.

Date - 28/03/2020

Till now I am achieving my plans although I am two to three days late as per my plan. But I am experiencing a change in me I can see that I am performing better from a previous time. Now I just have to maintain that consistency.
Sometimes I feel stressed also that time I imagine how happy I feel when I will pass and then I'll just study with full force sometimes I have to use motivational songs also to boost me when I feel tired.

After giving mock tests I realise my mistakes and work on them and improve them day by day honestly it is very difficult to maintain consistency but I have chosen this path and I will run on it no matter how effort it will take because this is my last chance to prove myself to me not others.

In the entire process, my mother is helping throughout the day she is giving the food on my table she always ask me do I need something.

Honesty this time I feel obsessed with my plans I never feel like procrastinating my work I just always want to do it as per my plan.

But for some days I also feel demotivated when I face my cousin making fun of me by giving unnecessary advice which is not required as per my situation he was doing just to make me realise that he is more knowledgeable than me.

whenever I feel I just try to ignore that negative person as much as possible and then I breathe and continue with my studies and forget whatever running in my mind because studying requires my hundred per cent focus which can be achieved by mental peace. For maintaining my calm I also watch some of my favourites shows they are the reward for me whenever I achieve my plans I reward myself with some pleasurable stuff with that I can maintain the balance off my mind till now my preparations are good.

Date - 10/5/2020

My exam will be in after 5days I am prepared but nervous at the same time my some concepts are a little bit weak also. But I am confident in what I know. I don't know whether the efforts I have made will be worth it or not because I can't say anything before exams. I isolated myself from others completely and the full day I only think for exams only. When I think that I can't do I start reminding myself of my past success and the face of my cousin brother.

Now I just have to maintain my physical health as well as mental health so that my health cooperates with me in exams. One thing I always kept in my mind is that I have to do this for my future self and my mother.

I can feel the butterfly in my stomach because the exams a too close and happy that after the exam I will feel very relaxed.
I always thought that if I just focus on my goal nothing else I will be able to compensate for all my past failures, sacrifices, because I have too much life ahead I cannot sacrifice today's hard work because of just petty pleasures.

But I never feel sad about it because I am lucky enough to study so why do I feel sad about it some people want to study but they don't have enough resources to study this is a harsh reality their aspirations, goals, motivation get suppressed under the externalities, I feel privilege that I have everything that is required to achieve my goal.

Date - 5/07/2020

Today was a big day for me I didn't sleep for a full night. Although I am confident still feel nervous. No one in my family is expecting much from me because of my past performances.

Full day I make sure that I stay away from my cousin brother who makes fun of me on my birthday and makes myself busy with some work. So that I don't think about my result. The result was declared at 3 pm but I got a notification on youtube that the results are out at 1 pm honestly, I don't have any fear because I don't have anything to lose I type my roll no. and suddenly BOOM "pass".

All failures, hard work, sacrifices, my never give up attitude just paid off. Then I saw the happiest face of my mother.

But honestly, I was expecting this to happen because I was passionate about the process this result is just a by product.
Still, I have some insecurity about my age so didn't post on any social media another reason is that there is one more level left so I don't want to make myself overconfident.

At night when I am writing about it, I learn that sometimes it is hard to accept reality, and it hits hard when you have not even thought of it, I never thought that being with a very good academic background I will face this phase of failures.

You just have to believe in yourself, life will always be unfair to you just have to deliberately create a chance of your success.
If you fail a couple of times now just stop and take the right decision and you don't need to lower your aim " provided you have the required skill for that ", rather make aim bigger than your previous one because it will give you a lot of energy to achieve it otherwise if you reduce your aim and continue to be in your comfort zone which will give you dissatisfaction.

There is nothing wrong with plan B but don't think about it until you give your 100%. If you leave just for the sake of it you will regret it for your entire life and regret hurts more than failure.

- Puneet Verma

KEERTHI L

Hey guys... This is KEERTHI L from Raichur, Karnataka. She is a spectrum writer at BOUNCE OVER EXPECTATION. She is pursuing her career in BAMS (Bachelor of Ayurvedic Medicine and Surgery). She loves to read books in her free time.

You can find her at.
Instagram ID : @silent scream.
Personal ID : @keerthi__09.

Simple things makes life more beautiful. Complex things creates only complications..

One Mistake

What was that MISTAKE??

Kiara was standing in the graveyard before her was the grave of her best friend. She was remembering that day when she lost everything, her 2 besties and her love

2 years ago.............

Kiara, Priya and Neha were childhood best friends. After completing their schooling they joined in the same college.

In the late winters as they were getting nearer to sports day they went to look around the play ground. They saw a football court but that not which caught their attention but they guys which were playing there. Particularly one guy, they kept staring at him for solid 10 minutes. To say he was handsome was an understatement. He was beyond handsome. They all got crush on the same guy.

After some stalking they got to know that he was Ankush, their senior, captain of college football team and also topper of college.

Now they started to talk to him. Among them Neha was not so much interested in him. Because, she was getting closer to Karthik, who was their classmate. They both were becoming serious about their relationship day by day. So Neha was out of the equation.

Now Kaira and Priya, Priya was liking him but not so much as Kaira, she was normally talking to him. Whereas Kaira was totally in love with him.

Ankush was very good guy with a hot body. He was star of the college. So many girls were happy by just getting him to talk to them. But he didn't like very desperate girls, he was disgusted of girls falling all over him.

He liked simple , normal and shy girls. That was exacting how we could describe Priya. That was the reason he was very drawn towards her. He liked to spend more and more time with her. Somewhere he was falling for her. On the other side Priya also started liking him. She enjoyed his company.

She also started spending time thinking about him.

Kaira was a bubbly type of girl. People liked to talk to her. She was very funny and easy to talk with good sense of humor. But she was very serious about Ankush.

In the beginning she ignored that Ankush saw her as a friend and he was head over heals for Priya. But ignoring that became hard when Priya was her best friend and Ankush was the guy she loves with her whole heart .

This all went to extreme level when Ankush went down on his knees and proposed Priya on valentine's day in a club full of people of their college.

Kaira's heart was broken. She was shread into pieces when she saw the guy she loves with everything she had going on his knees for her best friend.

Next day everyone in the college came to know that the famous Ankush was in a serious relationship. This was the hot topic in the college for many days.

Here Kaira was very jealous of her own best friend. She was ignoring Priya and Ankush both and started being alone but she was very disturbed and depressed. Crying herself to sleep was her daily routine. Priya and Neha both tried to talk to her but she was ignoring both of them.

One day she thought, this was not her depressed,silent, sad, crying. She was very strong girl. She thought that the root of her problem and sadness was her jealously towards Priya. Then she went to Priya and talked to her. They both started rebuilding their friendship. She even started behaving normal with Ankush . They both again friends.

As time passed everything started to become normal. One day Priya got a message from Ankush saying her to meet him in the locker room there is something important to talk. As she went to there, she found a shirtless, dripped in sweat very hot Ankush. He was in his under dressed state with the athletic storts, sports shoes and towel around his neck. When Ankush turned he was startled to see Priya there staring at him.

He smirked at her and started getting closer to her. When she was in a reachable distance he grabbed her by her waist and pulled her into a deep heart mealting kiss. Then one thing lead to another......

That was a beautiful time of there life. It was the first time they were so close to each other . They both wanted to treasure that moment. Both were very happy when they returned to their rooms that day. Next morning when Priya woke up smiling she didn't know taht her smile was not going to last long. When she went to college that day she got weird looks from whom ever she passed in the college. Neha came to her and pulled her to the corner. Priya asked Neha what's wrong with everyone. Neha gave her a sympathetic look and started digging for her phone. Then she opened some site and gave it to her. As Priya looked at the screen there it was the video of her and Ankush together in the locker room. The video was gone viral over night. Almost everyone in the college have seen that video.

Priya was standing there looking at her self in the video. She didn't understand what to do. She was panicked to the state that even though Neha was talking to her she couldn't here a word. She heard her name being called and saw Ankush rising towards her before she passed out .

Next day both Ankush and Priya were restricated from the college for their indecency in college premises. Priya didn't imagine in her 100 years that the beautiful time of her life will haunt her like a bad nightmare. She couldn't face her parents and world so she decided to end her life that night.

Next day she was found dead in her room. She hanged herself to death. When police started investigation they couldn't find who uploaded that video online. So they took help of the cyber crime. When they tracked the IP address what they found stunded everyone. When police investigated It was Kaira. Priya's best friend. When police investigated her she accepted that she recorded the video and uploaded it.

On that when she saw Ankush going towards locker room she took phone from his bag and texted Priya and deleted that from his phone. Then she recorded video of them both in locker room and uploaded it online that night. But she didn't think that Priya will commit suicide. Then she was published legally for her crime. Kaira was very sorry for her action. Because of her that big mistake she lost everything. Now Ankush for whom she took such big step wouldn't look at her. She even lost Neha too.

But the guilt and regret didn't leave her. Because of her one mistake she destroyed the life of so many people. Ankush in the other hand was sent to multiple counseling to bring back his stability of his mind.

He became normal after so many stages of therapy. But he was not able to erase the memories of Priya from his heart. Priya was like a beautiful dream in his life. After her death there was a void emptiness in his life. He was never able to love any other girl again..

- Keerthi L

VENKATESHWARARAO VADDADI

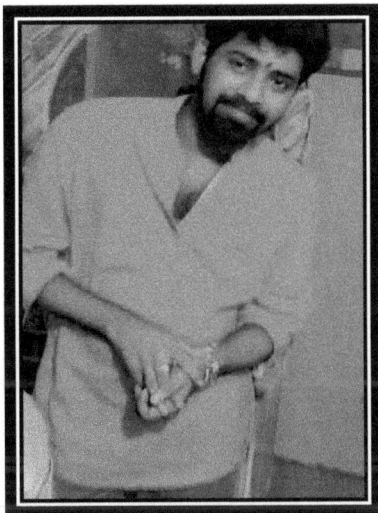

Venkateshwara Rao is highly passionate person with dreams and wants to make them real in his life with hardwork and great effort. He do not wish to set himself up as an example to Others but he want the readers not to make the same mistakes what he has done simply thinking it is easy to do it anything, without any knowledge and hardwork.
He believes "Continuous effort is the only shortcut and luck to your success".

Instagram ID : @call_me_by_venky

Story of My Life

I was born on March 8 1997. My parents named me with the name Venky. My father is serving in the government sector and my mother is a housewife and I have an older sister (Satya Lakshmi). Like every one, I also have a dream.

This story is about a boy. How he worked hard and made decisions to achieve his goal by working hard

I completed my schooling and intermediate in my home town. During my school days it's quite enjoyable and lovely with pure thoughts without any pressure. I encountered my setback after completion of my intermediate that is my entrance exam for my B. Tech. Like everyone I also want to go to good university and achieve good results and find a nice job and make my family lively and happy. But due to lack of resources and information required for exam I disappointed on myself. Due to my negligence and not know the value of marks didn't even tried to gather books for the exam. After completion of my exam the results are out .as expected I just qualified in the exam. With my scoring I know that I can't go to a good university, so I joined in management quota.

For my college studies, I needed to move from my home town to another place for further studies. This is my first time staying outside and study. At First I was very afraid at a thought how my college life will be in a new place with new people. Later after being with new friends the college days are smooth and enjoyable with my new friends. I stayed in my college hostel with school friends. The days moved so fast the day of graduation. I completed my graduation 4 years with some hard work and luck. In my 4 years study other than little knowledge about subject what I learned the most is how to survive in outside society how to support ourselves with the little money you have in your hands. And in hostel I have seen people with different personalities and different ideas. I learn mostly about how you should talk to people who came from different places and different backgrounds and how the people will change with time.

After graduation I have taken gap for 1 year to think what I want do and I am interested in. Everyone will have some magical skills and some talent and I also want to know what I am good at it. I have found that I have no magical skills and talent so I found that only with hard work you can survive in our society and make our parents and family to live a good life. So, I have to develop myself by changing the way I think. So I started thinking how to change my mind set.

How I changed my mindset

I thought, in order to achieve my goal in my life my biggest obstacle is my mind.

And I started to change the way I think and the choices I should take to get what I want.

I learned that life will test us with setbacks but these situations are not permanent.
We have full control of our choices to keep moving forward one step at a time.

I have learned that we all have reservoirs of unstoppable potential and can achieve great things by setting goals.

In order to achieve your goals definitely there will be lot of obstacles and walls you need to cross by your efforts and choices.

- Venkateshwara Rao

Problem Solving

How far you can go it depends on how you approach your problems and how you make your decisions to solve them.

You need to develop yourself continuously to get succeeded.

Even a marginal improvement in our process can have a huge impact on or end results.

You have to improve his decision success rate to make you have faith in yourself.

In order to complete the larger tasks you need to break them down to manageable tasks. During this process you may have doubt, fear, pain swirled in your thoughts but you must stay with patience.

Intended or meant means you can't get success. Core of success is not only the talent but also its efforts. And with the hard work I have done.

I have a job in IT field with It my financial need is supported for now. So the next task is to move for high position in your field. With higher efforts and hard work success may be late but you will succeed.

- Venkateshwara Rao

TJO

TSHEPO JOSEPH OLEBOGENG SEKETE is a budding writer at Spectrum Of Thoughts for anthology name – "Bounce Over Expectation". He holds Bachelor of Education in Economics. He hails from ' Rustenburg city in South Africa'. He enjoys drawing and writing.

You can find ' Him ' at
Instagram ID: @tjo_wries
Facebook   : TJO Poetry

Script

I was born with a script
They could reminisce about my future
I was either a junkie or mail man
I was a percentage increase in poverty
I was a potential criminal
I was an absent father
More especially I was good for nothing
I was another black child born in the system
The system designed by the whites for the whites
Born in a society intended to trap blacks
Trap them by scripting their lives long before their mother's pregnancy
They blind us to the possibility of seeing our full potential
They blind us from dreaming beyond our parents' visions for us
They blocked our vision of characters better than that in our community
The sky was the goal so they dug holes so that we start far behind
But every skyscraper has a basement floor
Thus I smiled because I knew what I was
While they thought they did

- Tjo

Slum Life

A lifestyle with more warnings than examples
Many characters warn you about who not to be
And only a few are examples of who to become
And the pressure to escape the lifestyle
But it's a crab jar
Escaping this life is almost a joke
But can be realised
The efforts to escape are countered by a friend
A foe masked as friend
Yes, they care about you
But they don't want to see you doing better
Unless they are already doing better
They love you but they hate to watch you win
It's a crab jar
Designed to keep us all inside
But the jar is full
And the crabs have had enough of the cluster
The jar is about to break
And the crabs will break free
I just pray the world is ready

- Tjo

The Rough

Dusty streets of rusty
Where most are born with a script
A rusty script that they should end up dusty
The script is rusty because it's been the story for most
A seed sawn in dust
An unbelievable marvel
Only water having been rain
The seed soared
A miracle was an understatement
A tree grew from dust
A steadfast tree
That can never be moved from its purpose
A tree with ripe fruits to feed nations
Who could have thought...
That trees also grow from dust?
I mean some seeds struggle to become on good soil
But the unbelievable Hope Tree was brought to pass on mere dust
From nothing to something
As is unbelievable that gold is initially just a stone
The heat turns it to gold
While most stones turn to nothing in hot conditions
Some turned in to metallic substances
Or how a piece of crystal can withstand unimaginable pressure
The very pressure that would crack big rocks
Somethings are just unexplainable but still very possible

- Tjo

Equations and Inequalities

The fortunate grab the attention
They become the ladies' man
They celebrate their wins without realising they are kind of a curse
Slums grow marvellous flowers
And the most fortunate get to pick and choose
This becoming their doom
They often make the mistake of exploring the garden
Ending up contacting deadly viruses
This system is cruel yet genius
The colour of your skin determines your future
If you're born with black skin, then you will have dark future
And if you have a white skin you get a bright future
But if you're destined for greatness you simply are
A black man has been way less than an unconsidered civilian
A black man has been way less than a pawn
But have you seen a black man shun the fight?
Have you seen a black man fail to smile?
Black skin is pure magic
And you can never deny that
Blacks are beautiful

-Tjo

Black Rose

Flowers are colourful
Flowers are bright
You were the exception
They thought you were a tree
But you looked like them
You possessed all their qualities
But they still didn't see you
They thought they knew better
That you're too different to be one of them
When in reality they feared you
They realised that you're a flower
Just more beautiful
And more daring
They thought your existence would kill their clout
And actually it wowed it
A black beautiful and thorny flower
Dark flowers are more attractive than your typical flowers
Who would could have thought?
A mere difference in colour
Can evoke such unnecessary contention

- Tjo

SHARAD JHA

Sharad Jha is from Araria, Bihar. He is highly passionate towards to write quotes, poetry and story

Mail ID : sharadprna123@gmail.com

Bounce Over Expectation

Once I met someone who seemed very ordinary in appearance. Both of us were going to the same place order from the train he sat on the next to me. But there was a strange smile on the face of the stranger, it seemed that something untoward had happened to him. I tried to ask him something but he did not reply anything, I tried to ask again from time to time, he is so much in response. His answer was that now I will not expect anyone again. I did not understand sitting that stranger, I asked him to tell the whole situation but he was afraid to tell but I told him there is no such thing as panic. I should give some courage to that stranger so that he can tell his whole story. He showed a slight smile on the face of the stranger, it seemed that he had been talking to someone for a long time was ready to tell his whole story but there were tears in his eyes too. Stranger told that there is no reality like real life movie, it is not a fiction.

This stranger began to tell his story, he tell that once he met a person, he was very innocent in appearance, the stranger whom he met. That person told his story to the stranger, he is alone in the world, he has no one, because of this, the stranger took that person with him to his house and kept him.

The person who helped, he belongs to the rich family. After staying for a few days in the house of bud richer person, his mind was born out of greed. One day that person mad a plan with some person, how to steal all the goods, finally the plan was prepared. Richer person had gone out one night, on the same night he had to give the result of this plan. There were some people in the house like his family. The person who had come with the intention of stealing killed all the people of his family and stole the essence and ran away when richer person returned home the next day seeing all this, his confidence was lost from all. Richer person's more faith took everyone's life.

Don't want to help without knowing about anyone......

OVER EXPECTATION KILLS

-Sharad Jha

TEESHA AURORA

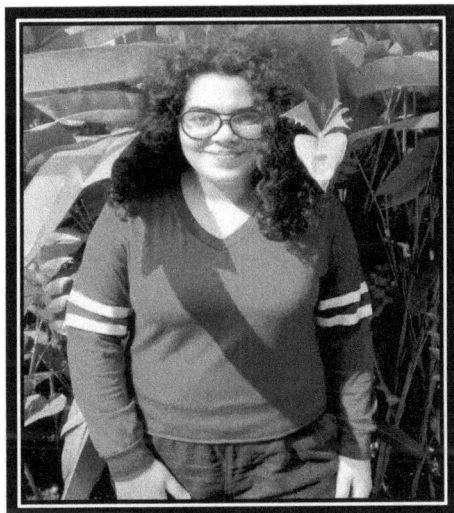

Teesha is a sixteen-year-old pursuing humanities at Jamnabai Narsee School. She has been writing since the fifth grade with the hope that her poetry can allow someone to feel a sense of familiarity in a world that seems to grow increasingly strange.

You can find her at
Instagram ID : @wordsandverses_ta!

Expect

You ask me where I feel the pressure
I feel it in my shadow and by that I mean it's barely there
I could escape it with ease if I ran far enough
at the time I didn't know that my grey friend could turn into my doom
otherwise I would have scurried to the ends of the earth

What I wanted from life at the time was simple
I wanted fresh grass to play on
I wanted my best friend to come and paint with me
I wanted my parents to take me to the mall every other Sunday and when
i grew up i wanted to be like the nice uncle at the park who gave me free
ice-cream
there is an unadulterated joy that one experiences at seven
there is an innocence to it, and there is the beauty
of being conscious of what is going on around you
but not being expected to act like you recognize it all the time
I wish I could go back to seven
to yellow swings in the park
and skies the colour of my favourite teddy bear
I was expected to be happy, carefree, irresponsible, and it was okay if I
laughed too loudly or cried too much
I was okay being me

-Teesha Aurora

Crumble

You ask me where I feel the mounting pressure
I point to the back of my gut and the sides of my throat
it is when these parts are full that I feel the most empty
I did not want to be this way
succumbing to my survival instincts, doing anything to survive in a
society that only sees in me the money I can make
they don't want me awake
I think growing up kills you

When I was younger, I had dreams, passions, I had hope
I was alive
I wrote poetry for my lover at 2 in the morning
I fought for what I believed in
I loved my friends fiercely
I wanted to live in one of those glass buildings in the heart of the city
I don't know what society has made me

I wake up in the morning and I check my phone
Life is beginning to feel like cause-effect-cause-effect-decay
I don't feel like I am in control
my actions are dictated by what you say

'That's an unflattering shirt to wear'
'That's a weird thing to study'
'That's a stupid way to walk'

I have twisted and turned every inch of myself to fit into your mould
what else can you expect from me but to be scared, to be horrified of how
much more I am going to have change
who I am ,I have barely begun my life and I am already scared of what is
to come
How can I write poetry when I am expected to pick up calls when I am
driving
because my car connects to my phone
How can I fight for what I believe in when the only reason I got here in
the first place was conformity,
Was keeping my mouth shut
How can I talk to my best friend when she's in a different time zone and I
don't care enough to stay up till 3 am and neither does she
How can I live in the glass buildings when they rest on me making so
much money that
I feel like an immoral person but this pressure keeps building up

Be romantic, be strong, be kind, be famous, be the best at everything you
do
I just want to be me
I just want to live
How can I ever be happy under your sneering gaze
Your expectations hurt like a knife to the chest

-Teesha Aurora

Discover

You ask me where I feel the pressure
I say I feel it at this spot at the front of my forehead
It's always there but it has become easier to ignore
I have always wanted different things from life
but reality is a cruel, cruel mistress
So I learnt to make life my own in the time I had left

Who cares for glass buildings and money
When I have a home whose every corner is filled with art and love
Who cares about parties and luxury
When my lover makes me tea in the morning and always lets me sleep for
an extra 5 minutes
Who cares about the clubs and the roaring music
When my friends come over every Thursday for game night and my best
friend always sits next to me
Who cares about cool cars and cooler houses
When I am beginning to find home in myself

I don't care about this superficiality and pretty dresses and beautiful
dresses and porcelain sculptures
They are meaningless until I have someone to appreciate them with

I didn't grow up exactly how I expected and maybe it was for the best
I don't feel like I need anything more from life than warm tea, the knick
knacks that litter my shelf, and the people I love

This is enough, this is good, and this is the dream
I am beginning to be me again

-Teesha Aurora

SHREYA RAI

Hey! I am Shreya rai. I love to write because I think it's best way to present your feelings.

miss__attitude__3082

Apart from our families we all have a special person to whom we give a special place in our hearts. Though we don't share blood relation with each other but we have strong bond between us connected to our hearts.

This person always stands by you and supports you to the fullest . They may know your strength and weakness but they never take advantage of your weakness. They always try to make you grow more stronger than before.

Not only this they care like a mother, they handle your tantrums like a father, they love you like a sister, they fight with you like a brother. We can say that we get a whole family in one person. They are too trust worthy even we can share our secrets with them.

Did you all come to know about whom I have been talking about? Yes, you guessed right. I am talking about that person who was only a stranger to me before but now she had become an important part of my life and holds a special place in my heart. She is no one but my best friend to whom I call monkey, witch, idiot with love.

In this fake world if you get a best friend who makes you feel special, who understands you, loves you, become your backbone in your no-win situations. Then nothing can be amazing than this.

Before I met this gorgeous my life was incomplete. It's not like I was not happy and doesn't know how to enjoy the life. I use to do all those things. But when this girl took entry in my life she made my life more beautiful. She taught me how to enjoy the life to the fullest. She filled colours of joy and happiness in my life. She made my life too easy to live. She helps me to deal with my problems and also she helps in my studies.

Here I came to know why do we people call this person as, our best friend. Why not just a friend? We call them best friend because they always do their best for us. They give their best advice to you and they make you to be best. They not only be a part of your celebrating moments but they stand by you in your critical situations.

Friendship is a relation which is completely different from other relations. It is beautiful relation between two people. Who understand each other? The bond is too strong that even they can see hidden tears behind a beautiful fake smile .

If you have a friend who says why do you worry? I am here for you. Then you are truly blessed. These peoples are really gem. They become happy on your success and celebrate your success as their success. But this people are somewhat typical they are always ready to take treat from you but not to give. They never forget your birthday, but they never call you or text you to wish they call you to ask for the party. This people are not going to change.

Don't know how but she turned to be more than a best friend. She has become too close to me that I can't even imagine my life without her. She is too naughty but before my parents she becomes a girl full of sacraments. There's no match to her acting of descent behaviour. And then I have to listen see how polite she is learning something from her. But I know the reality.

Our bond is too strong that it cannot be broken by any misunderstanding. The trust which we both have on each other becomes a protective shield to our relationship. Try to build your bond too strong that no third person should dare to break your bond.

To make any relationship strong trust is very important. Until trust exists relationship exist. The day you lose your trust relationship breaks into pieces. To make any relationship successful efforts should be put by both the sides and this will make your bond stronger.

Have you ever thought what is friendship? And how a best friend should be? If you take my opinion I would say a best friend is who feel happy when you laugh, who hate tears in your eyes, and never feels jealous of your success or something else. Because when jealous comes in between it breaks the relation. A devoted friend will never get jealous of their friend's happiness.

And I am lucky enough to have a friend like her who poses all those qualities which a best friend should have. If you have this kind of people in your life please let them not walk out of your life.

A true friend becomes your teacher when you need correct guidance. They will never let you to walk on wrong path. They will always show you right direction. They oppose you if you are wrong and also try to make you understand that you are wrong. They do this without hurting you.

I am glad to say that I'm abundantly blessed to have a friend like this. A good friend always appreciates you and encourages you to step forward. Not only this sometimes they make you aware of your hidden talents.

I am thankful to God, that he gifted me a monkey in a structure of human being. Who take great care of me and loves me?

"People fell in love but I fell in friends love"...

R.PRIYADARSHINI

R.Priyadarshini is a budding writer at spectrum of thoughts for Frantic confession. I'm studying 12th at Zion matriculation higher secondary School, madambakkam. I'm from Chennai. I enjoy pursuing writing Tamil poetry during the free hours.

Priyadarshiniraj1910@IG

Aruyir friend.

You are not proud to have a thousand friends, you should be proud to say that the one who travels with you for your boundless love is the one who will never give up on you even if a thousand people oppose you!

Pride of friendship.

You will be my support in my happiness and your support in my misery. If I have a victory flag, you will be happier to celebrate than I am. The only true companion is to hold hands so that I will be in any pain and situation!

The beauty of friendship.

The bond available to all the souls born in this world will not be reciprocated by my friend. even if the best friend gives a thousand crores to me it will not be satisfied. Because the happiness that my friend gives will never be more than equal to the happiness that a thousand crores can give! The difference is not that one is not born in a womb but that the soul is united even though it is differentiated by the body.

MEHREEN FIRDOUS

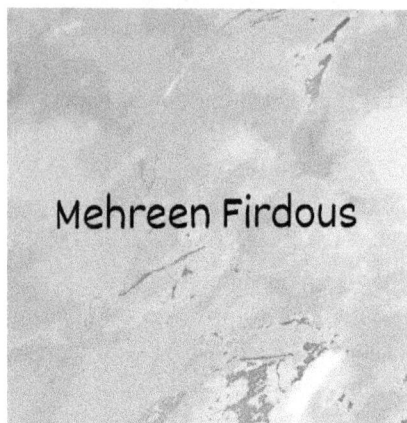

Hi.. I'm Mehreen Firdous. I turned 18 this April. I love writing, it makes me happy. My favourite quotes these days is "She believed she could, so she did".

mehreen._firdous@IG

Friendship is a special gift

Do you know, what's the best feeling in the world?

Yes you're right! Having friends, with whom you can share anything and everything is literally the best feeling in the world.

When it comes to friends, they have a very special place in our life, which is Irreplaceable.

As, friends are the family, we choose for ourselves.

Apart from our families, friends play a vital role in shaping our life. As they are the ones, who accept you the way you are. They know everything about you - they're aware of your flaws, but still, they adore you for being what you are! Because of them, we laugh a little harder, cry a little less and smile a lot more. Having friends at every stage of our life, is both bless and bliss as they are the ones, who loves you without conditions, they will be always there for you - to guide you, to support you, to encourage you and to make you realise your worth. They're the ones who believes in you even when you can't believe in yourself.

Friendship is a sweet responsibility, a pure relation connected by souls. As friends are the crazy people who always listen to your crap, who make you feel home, when you're away from home.

It's difficult every time,

To be with someone in their difficulties.

From hiding their tears, to making us smile.

Only friends have this super power to make us laugh when we don't even want to smile.

Laughing until our stomach hurts, its what friends are for!

A true friend is someone, who enlightens your entire life - who will love you like a mother, guide you like a father, speak to you like a sister and argue with you like a brother.

Sometimes talking to your friend is the only therapy you need.

From an alarm to a reminder,

A bench mate to a philosopher,

A friend to a family....

They've lived most of our lives.

Friendship is a connection of heart and soul, where you don't need to change yourself to be with someone, you can be yourself.

Though we don't share any blood relation with friends, but still friendship is the strongest and most elegant relation in the world.

The relation where you need not to trust, you can believe. Where you need not to explain, you will be understood.

Side by side or miles apart

Friends will always be connected by heart.

When you think of memories you've made with your friends,

Those memories become treasures.

Every moment spent with friends becomes a sweet memory - we didn't realise we were making memories; we were just living the moment.

From fighting with you for silly reason,

To loving you without any reason.

Friends are the crazy people, whose love is un-matched. They have magic to change your life, just by being in it.

Life is worth living, when you have friends who doesn't only understand your words, but also understand your silence. Moments spent with friends become great memories to last a lifetime. They become Irreplaceable part of our life - as they share our happiest moments, they listen to our saddest stories and they tell us when we are being stupid without fear that we will get upset.

Wonderful friends make wonderful days and unforgettable memories.

Friendship is the purest relationship - where you will be heard, without even speaking. You will be understood without explaining. It's one of the greatest bonds, anyone can never wish for. It's a devoted relationship between two Individuals. It is shared by two people who have similar interests and feelings.

A person is acquainted with diverse people in their life. However, the closest one become our friends. Having a true friend makes our lives easier and full of happiness. In a true friendship, a person can be themselves completely without the fear of being judged. It makes you feel loved and accepted. There is no greater feeling in the world than having a friend who is loyal to you.

From sharing stories,

To stealing chocolates.

Friendship holds significant stature in life as it teaches unforgettable life lessons, some valuable lessons that will change your life, how to love others apart from family.

It is a relationship that grows stronger in time and holds a special place in our heart.

There is a definitive moment in a person's life where they know that they have found their partner in crime.

The person they can count on to be awkward with.

Yes, that awkward person, happens to be our friend.

Friends give us the absolute privilege and honour of being able to call them our friend. They give us these reasons and a million more to be thankful for.

From,

A complete stranger.

To,

Our best friend,

Soulmate,

Secret keeper,

Another half,

Human dairy and

Personal advice!

Friends turned to be our everything.

They have the ability to make ordinary moments, extraordinarily delightful. A simple day can become special because of them. They deal with our Immaturities and tantrums. They never fail to make us laugh. There's never a dull moment with them.

Friends are like the best assets of our life because they share our sorrow, sooth our pain and make us feel happy.

They never create bad times, Instead, give one the best memories to live upon.

They teach you to understand and trust people. However, friends are not related by blood, but they are related by love.

Friendship teaches the importance of loyalty and reliability. There is no greater feeling in the world than a loyal, trustworthy friend by your side. However, friendship isn't a one-way path to experience loyalty and trust; one needs to return the mutual feelings to complete the circle of friendship.

Therefore, friendships are real-time connections.

Friendship isn't a word, it's an emotion relished with trillions of memories!

ISHITA BHATTACHARYA

I am a marketing professional, who is passionate about writing. I also, have a blog where I write about the recent marketing trends and updates http://www.reachcreativelyyours.com/. If you like my story and want me to write more or you have some suggestions for improvement do write back to me @ishitab.mail@gmail.com. "Creation is addictive, I love creating".

Gauri Bakes – The Kitchen Story

"Ria come to the kitchen" – her mom called. She hated this time of the day, disliked stepping foot in the kitchen. She did not like the hot moist air in the kitchen, the hot utensils, the chopping board, the knife she hated everything in the kitchen. More than that she disliked arranging things in place and cleaning the kitchen. But her mom has decided to teach her cooking and to take care of the most important room of the house "THE KITCHEN". "After all, post your marriage, you need to take care of your kitchen so learn from now. Only if you know how to work you can instruct others to work" told her mother "Even if you have maids, you need to guide them or make them work. So, at the end you should have the expertise". She had no other choice but to come to the kitchen. It was one of those ordered which cannot be disobeyed.

She was smart enough, some days she managed some external help or had important task at hand to finish to dodge her kitchen timing duty. She ran either to her father or grandfather, or she has her urgent homework to complete. "If you do not learn now you will repent in the future" – Shouted her mother in anger whenever she managed to escape the kitchen duty.

Her grand mom patiently observed all these family dramas. That day it was her Ria's brothers' birthday. It was the tradition of the house that cake will always be baked in house and not ordered. As grandma was the best cook, she baked the cake always. Even that day she planned for the cake. She called Ria and asked her to help her with beating the egg "My hand is paining today, may be the arthritis pain again. Help me beat the egg, butter, and sugar well together. Let me teach you"- said grandma. Ria was always ready to help her grandma she came down and helped her in the cake preparation. Little did she know that it was such an easy and enjoyable work. Her efforts were gratified with a dark chocolate cube and the tempting smell of the baked cake at the end of the hard work. She was overjoyed when the cake was served to her brother. She felt the joy of creation in her. The happiness in her brothers' eyes, the soft cake which melted her mouth, the sweet aroma which filled the air in the house filled her with contentment. Post this day, helping her grandma in preparing cake had become her hobby. Little did she realize that she had started enjoying the process and would visit the kitchen often. Slowly one day she had started baking cake herself and grandma had become her helper. When this role reversal happened, it was difficult to say. But it was easy to say that she baked one of the best cakes which her friends and families waited to munch on. Not only grandma was even successful in teaching her prepare all her favourite food, luchi, pulao, fried rice, pantua etc. Slowly, days passed and the girl who hated stepping foot in her kitchen one day, bakery of her own.

The bakery has franchise chain across India and one of the top-rated chains in all portals. The speciality of her chain is her grandma style vanilla cake. It has been the top seller and has been able to create it mark across geographies and culture. She has named her store as "Gauri Bakes" her as tribute to her best friend her grandma. She is a successful professional too working as "Marketing Head" in a multinational company. She has been able to successfully manage both are responsibilities. After her marriage she had realised that being a woman the only value that was appreciated in her was her culinary skills. She has to answer the question to almost everyone "Beti you stay alone? Do you know to cook?" even in her office she has been asked this question by both the male and female colleagues. She always replied with a smile "Yes, can cook for survival". At this age she realised why her mom tried to teach her. It is not the professional achievement that a woman is appreciated for it is her culinary skills which needs to be honed to be called a perfect woman. Kitchen is a place she cannot hate to go. But Ria still hates going to the kitchen even today, she only cooks when she feels like, she only cooks those food she is passionate about. She loves to do those things she enjoys. This her grandma has understood long back, hence she taught her the way she would enjoy, and not feel cooking as a punishment or torture. Today when she manages her family, profession, and own start up like with pride, she missed her grandma the most. There is no one today who would understand her the way she is. No one will understand her needs, her happiness and her interests, her unsaid needs only her best friend could.

She has always aimed to be a top-rated business owner and be covered by top magazines. She has been able to achieve that and lot more. She has been able to achieve that and lot more with her best friend by her side always like a support pillar. A space which never can be filled.

V.SURIYA PRABHA

Suriya prabha was a medical student. She started her insta page q.u.o.t.e.s_41 and shared her thoughts. As a medical student she thought mental health is most important. Her writings were based on motivation and determination. She believed motivation enhances our mental health. During her school days,she came across a betrayal done by her close friends and when she lost faith in friendship, a girl proved her the definition of friendship. So, she would like to share a thank note to her. q.u.o.t.e.s_41@IG

A Letter To My Friend

(I am your piggy; you are my doggy)

This is my indirect confession to my friend because she's not that dramatic and feels it cheesy.

Friend, the short word that made me long for it and took a long way to reach me.

Initially, I too had friends, but when they betrayed me, when no one stood with me during my hard times and when they left me after they found a new one, I lost faith in friendship and decided,

"It's better to be alone than to be left alone".

After that, I started enjoying my own company. Many have called me selfish, arrogant and stone-hearted.

"Yeah, I'm stone hearted, looking for a chisel to shape my heart.".

Just because I'm on my own doesn't mean I'm an introvert. I love hanging out with people. But I set a boundary around me. A lot of people tried to cross it, but I didn't have the confidence to let them in. Whatever the situation is, life goes on right?. Still, my heart yearned for someone to conquer my trust.

"Trust is like an opportunity, once lost, it's difficult to gain it again."

I wasn't really close to her at the beginning. Great things take time right? Later, we became so close. I don't know how, when? Why?. But it happened. That may be because of her sense of humour. She's great at making others happy.

Her words and actions have never hurt anyone. But she made me jealous. I thought I found my chisel, but it was busy crafting someone's heart. .

   "Jealousy is also a sign of friendship"

But she knows how to balance the friendship.

She never ignored me for others.

The moment when she conquered my trust:

I was punished for being talkative and told to stand before the class. But she voluntarily accepted the punishment and accompanied me as she thought I might be left alone there. At that point, the door of my border opened for her. Since then, we have shared not only our punishments, but also our happiness and sorrows. She became my diary. I started sharing my daily events with her. My day starts with her and ends with her. Our journey started as a stranger to friend to best friend and now we are more than best friends.

"We are soulmates"

"Best friends share their
Happiness and sorrows.
Soulmates no need of
Words to express it.

Best Friends have
Photos together.
Soulmates have
Memories together.

Best Friends have
Same wavelength.
Soulmates may have
Different wavelength
Yet shine like a rainbow."

I didn't envy her other friends anymore. As I know I was her priority. But others got jealous of us. I started to learn the definition and importance of friendship. I realised that friendship is all about giving instead of getting. I started to care about others too.

From a single person to now I have a gang to rely on. But she's always my special person.

"Our friendship is like a

Ship with an anchor

Never slips away."

I am a little short-tempered. I got frustrated, even for the small matters. That's one of the bad habits I have. But I'll figure it out in a few minutes. But it takes more time for others to forgive me.

"Anger is like a boomerang"

But, she never showed it back. She coped with me even before I did. Maybe that's her character and I started to learn it.

One day, there was a demise in her family. She got too depressed and we only had a short conversation that week. But it showed how depressed she was. Like iron and magnet, our emotions are tied to each other. Her happiness made me happy, her depression made me depressed.

"Yes, we are interconnected."

If you get something

After so many hurdles

You'll know the importance of it.

You'll be afraid of losing it.

So, I have a nightmare that,

'Will we be the same after graduation? '

But, I promise you that.

"We may take different paths.

They may be far apart.

But our friendship

Will never fall apart."

I hope that years later, even after our teeth begin to fall, our hair becomes grey and even when our eyesight becomes blurry, we still read this confession and laugh together. Love you doggy.

TEHMINA SHAIK

Hi, this is Tehmina Shaik, I was told to write something about me, but let's just pretend I wrote something extra-ordinary Alhamdulillah and now smile :) [please co-operate with me]; Azhakallahu Sinnaka - May Allah swt keeps you smiling

_tehminashaik@IG

Safe & Ease

I find myself lost in my own company,

Fading into darkness and overthinking,

my miseries drag me into the puddle of mud,

I can't come out,

I can't seem to function

and then HE comes,

and his gentle voice keeps

my neck above the mud,

I come back,

rise again,

flourishing,

radiating and safe into his arms

and my heart is at

complete ease...

Ignorance Is Indeed A Bliss

I'm not ignoring you,

 I'm just keeping

myself from you,

so, I don't cling to

your beautiful soul

that loves a day or two

and leaves in the end...

'him'

I get jealous

of those beautiful eyes

that gets to

see Him

and I don't.

Growth

'I seem to water all my love

to you in the days

I don't even love myself

and that's my Love,

is problematic.'

  'Is it really a problem?'

'No, not really

because you gave me all

  the love I crave and need

Things I'd do for 'You'

My love,

  I don't deserve someone as

  naive as you.

  Please stop being okay with

  everything I do,

  you, my love,

  deserve to be treated right

  You deserve kisses on your forehead,

warm hands to hold,

[while I keep running away//]

You deserve firm shoulders to lean

on; little surprises, dinner

made with love, neck massages

if only you give me a chance,

I vow, my love.

I won't dishearten your heart...

I love you through my prayers.

      He has no idea how much

      I pray for him,

      his hifazah (protection),

      his maghfirah (forgiveness),

      and his future.

      [literally 'everything'.]

RESHMA BALIVADA

Hello everyone. My name is Reshma Balivada, and I am 18 years old. So, this is my very first story... I enjoy writing quotes and stories because they make me feel better. My emotions are transferred in the form of my quotes and stories.

_____.ms.barbie._____@IG

Everyone Stays In Your Good Time But Only Few Stays In Your Difficulties Too.

Hello, my name is Anaya.

This is an unpredictable storey from my life that I'd like to share with you. I had a lot of great friends up until this point, and then I met this person who never left my side and was always there for me in my worst hours. She is the sort of person that is extremely reserved and hence only speaks to a small group of people. Her interlocutor are her own loved ones. Our insanity has a lot in common... we both want to hang all the time. We met by coincidence in the EARLY DAYS OF COLLEGE LIFE, and we immediately grew to admire one other and were good friends... EVERYONE ON THE BACKBENCH HAD A GREAT TIME, INCLUDING US. SO, here's my story.... She was my entire universe. She is, in my view, the most gorgeous girl on the globe. She has a wonderful physical look. We were so close that we could understand one other just by gazing at each other. We quickly began to accumulate a significant quantity of memories. We were overjoyed to be best friends instead of friends. This was known throughout the campus. As previously said, both of us were backbenchers, implying that we are both extremely lazy. There were exams coming up, and we both used to sit on the last bench and relax! We were never interested in studies; all we did was eat, sleep, chat, and repeat. As our friendship strengthened, we began to go out! Beaches, restaurants, and so forth... we both had a great time every time. There was no third thing with us. We were both only concerned in ourselves. We adored one other in a way that even persons who had known each other for eight years couldn't. We had a lot of memories that will last a lifetime. The time we spent together was brief, but the memories and moments we shared were memorable. The nicest thing about her was that she used to treat me like a child.! Exams were always the villains in our pleasant days, and we failed to combat them! .. we proceeded from the top section to the bottom section. We both didn't enjoy it, but we had to do it since unexpected things happen all the time! I used to be someone who talked to everyone, but there is only one person who means anything to me is my love. Shruthi was a kind of person who only talked to a few people, and those few people were her loves! (But she does love me more than everyone else.)

We both walked upon Sravya, who was sitting alone on the bench! She reminded me of Shruthi... Sravya was a fun girl! We really had two more fools. rithu and saranaya... we five formed a group! Promised each other not to go no matter what... yet vows don't last long! and circumstances aren't always the same.

We were separated into two main sections in the second face of our college life: one for me, Saranya, and Sravya, and another for Rithu and Shruthi together. We were all fine with it because the only difference was the size of the class. There may be disparities in places, but our hearts are inextricably linked, and we can hardly believe it.

Meanwhile, Deepthi, whom we had never met, entered our lives, not ours, but mine, and changed everything...

In the meantime, I became close to Sravya. We each shared each other secrets... And all the difficulty began, slwoly as time went, Shruthi gradually stopped talking to me, whereas she used to cast a grin at me as if I were a stranger to her every time we met in college. I was devastated by her emotions since I had not expected such attitude from her.

So, I decided to question her about her conduct since I wanted her... Her only reaction was those unresolved questions, unexpressed feelings, and my gloomy thoughts...

She never entirely answered my inquiries, but she was constantly in a quandary, asking me to choose between love and conflict. She constantly placed me in a predicament where I had to decide whether Shruthi was mine or Deepthi's.

This type of circumstance was unanticipated!

Life is so unexpected, isn't it?

These sorts of incidents occur in everyone's life. Friendship is really important for everyone. But it was really essential for me since the relationship I had with Shruthi was very difficult to ignore, but I had to because she never exhibited any type of value to me.

I never anticipated to be devastated by her... I felt as if my life had no other option than to revolve around her. However, my friend Sravya altered my entire mindset, and she truly changed me.Sravya used to be with me in every scenario... not only her, but the entire gang was with me... we gradually lost contact with Shruthi... although we didn't get disconnected completely, but we did lose touch.

Not only did I feel awful, but everyone in our gang did since at some point or another, everyone was linked with her... but we chose not to be sorry about her issue and spoil our college lives. and decided to move on. Moving on, on the other hand, is not simple for me.

I used to merely gaze at her stuff or at her while she was with Deepthi! It took me a long time to adjust to life without her, but I always had her memories.

Sravya and I grew so close in such a short period of time! There were days when I didn't think of Shruthi at all. Sravya taught me to believe in myself, and she taught me to be obsessed with myself... Sravya quickly grew quite close to me. I gradually began to forget about Shruthiii.

But then there was that day when I fell from the bench and injured my nose and lips... I was so lucky that the entire class became concerned about me, and there was this one girl who didn't give a damn! SHRUTHI. I wept myself to sleep only for her. My pals Made Shruthi come to me after putting in a lot of work, and there goes our biggest conflict...

I argued with her, begging her to be just mine, not deepthis... I had a feeling deepthi wasn't right for her, but she was obstinate and she left the room as well as me... and there I was, standing in the room filled with gloom (much like my life), all alone and shattered. I went on, never looking back. But I shattered my heart in the scenario, and I wasn't in the mood to go back, and then this lovely lady Sravya changed everything...She altered my heart! She absolutely fixed me up and I had no idea she would become my best companion; I can proudly say she wasn't my buddy, but she was like my sister! Always there for me.

OUR INTERMEDIATE WAS COMPLETED. WE LEFT COLLEGE WITH BOTH BEAUTIFUL AND BROKEN MEMORIES...

Our gang was divided apart. Everyone went to separate colleges; we considered coming together but were unable to do so. We always missed our long conversations and the joy we used to have.

You are aware that my life has changed drastically. Sravya was with me the entire time. She used to look after me and spend meaningful time with me. and she quickly became my sibling.

Shruthi became my past as time passed, but my hopes never died. But our love died a long time ago, and I just recognised it recently.

sravya,rithu,saranya on that point, I'd want to express my heartfelt gratitude. thank you for making me a bteer person, three of you were with me the entire time and supported me in every situation...

Finally, I recognised and informed myself that...Everyone sticks with us when things are going well. However, only a few individuals remain in our terrible times, and they are the genuine people. because everyone needs happiness, but only a few people can turn melancholy into happy, and they are my dumb pals Thank you for sticking with me and keeping every promise you made.

VAIBHAVI

Writing is the painting of voice, this is Ruhi, my Wattpad account @pages_of_prose_

saranghae__7@IG

The Gift Of Love

- A true love story

EVERYONE, do you know what I hate the most, it's when classes are over. Wherever I go people start gossiping about me.

As I start walking in the corridor I heard so many whisperings around me.

"That's her? She was dumped by Aman" someone said, as the other replied by saying "she is not that pretty, I understand why he dumped her!"

I don't understand why people love gossiping. I know you are also curious about my story. So, what happened between me and Aman?

Oh! I didn't introduce myself did I? I'm Anjali, 18 years old, studying in Xavier's college 3rd-year arts.

6 days back

Aman, the most handsome hunk of our college, he is good at studies, sports, dancing what not ooh I should mention he is good at flirting too, that was one of the reasons why we broke up. He is good at flirting with other girls while already having a girlfriend(me). Speaking of which, he flirted with so many girls in front of me, and when I asked about his dirty behaviour he used to just cut it all by saying I'm possessive. It continued for a year and a half and then one fine day he entered our class, came to me, he stood in front of my desk, he cleared his throat "AHEM" by that the attention of whole class shifted to us both and then he said "LET'S BREAK UP, I CAN'T BEAR YOU ANYMORE, IT'S OVER" saying that he turned around and walked out of our class.

I was in shock until he left our class, I was like "What the hell just happened?" It was then I realized I was dumped, which should happen the other way, I should be the one to dump him, I was the most perfect girlfriend he could ever have!!! I wrote so many assignments for him, I completed his projects, I never flirted, or at least I never had a crush on celebrity while being in a relationship with him, how the hell he could do this.

It hurt my pride, I couldn't take it so I stood up from my seat and I walked to him firmly, showing off my confidence I called him "Aman, can I have a word with you" He turned towards me, holding a basketball in his right hand and he nodded, implying me to continue and I started speaking very boldly, in a way that amazed me "AMAN!! How dare you insult me What do you think? You are the most handsome man in our college, if so you are an idiot thinking so, cause you look like a pig, you eat like a pig, you do everything like a pig, so better call yourself a pig rather you idiot, you are basically a coward and don't even get me started with your attitude, despite all I am the one who has the right to break up with you, so listen carefully you moron, I'm breaking up with you, you said you can't bear me, the truth is you are unbearable, you flirt with every girl in our college you are such a dumb pig, see I will have a boyfriend who is more handsome more intelligent and most importantly more loving and loyal than you in 1 week." Saying that I turned my head and left the corridor and walked straight into the washroom, it took me nearly 5 mins to process the bullshit I said to him, what the hell, what do I do now? A new boyfriend, I must be dreaming. I look like a potato who the hell will love me and that too in 1 week, I'm doomed, what do I do now?

There were a lot of thoughts running through my head as I walked out of the washroom and then a miracle happened, I saw my saviour, the only one who can help me in this facade, my childhood buddy, my idiot monkey RAHUL as soon as I saw him I ran to him screaming "RAHULLLLLLLLLL!!" he saw me with a puzzled look on his face, I dragged him to a closed room and said about my breakup with Aman.

"Thank god you both got separated, I told you a trillion times that he is a playboy and he is not the right one for you, but you never listen to me, do you," said Rahul. I got tears in my eyes and in less than a minute they were unstoppable and I hugged him, he patted my back and said "whatever happened was for good, don't bother about him anymore" and then there comes the real matter that worried me the most, I told him about my challenge and he was shocked as hell. He started shouting at me "why did you do that!!!" He was so angry at me and he has all the rights I always create problems and always get me out of them, but this time I don't know!!! He shouted at me aggressively saying "Anjali, you are not a small child, get a hold of your bloody tongue, how the hell you challenged something impossible, you disappointed me, don't expect help from me this time" saying that he left the room, I'm back all alone, now what will happen?

It passed 6 days, I just have 1 day left, I don't know what to do, wherever I go I hear people whispering about me, they say mean things to me, thinking about all those I entered our library, where I heard some girls gossiping, I stood right behind the rack where they were chatting, "Do you know? Anjali is a gold digger, I heard that Aman paid for all the shopping Anjali did" said a girl and other replied saying "poor Aman, he went through a lot" "I would certainly kill myself if I hurt such a sweetheart(Aman) ever" another girl spoke.

It was humiliating, why am I the one who is listening to all the bull shit when I did nothing wrong, I sat there crying for no idea how many hours until I heard someone footsteps coming towards me, it sounded more like running, I didn't care but then I heard someone calling me "Anjali" I turned my head and then I saw Rahul standing there actually panting trying to catch his breath.

Why are you here? It's past college hours and I was searching for you the whole town, I messaged you so many times, I tried calling you 100 times, why didn't you lift my calls, you idiot. I went to your home to check but you were not even at home, why the hell are you here?" Rahul screamed at me.

I was shocked for a second seeing Rahul here and I asked him "why are you here Rahul?" "of course, for you Anjali, I was worried as hell about you?" Rahul exclaimed, hearing that my heart melted, its almost 8 pm and here is my Rahul who came to college searching for me, no one took care of me as Rahul does. When I was 6 years old my parents died in a car accident and from then I was living with my grandmother, though my granny took good care of me I always missed my mother and fathers love and affection until Rahul came into my life, he has always protected me like a father and cared for me like a mother, all the incidents and those beautiful memories from my childhood came in front of my eyes, and in every memory, there was Rahul with me.

I ran to him and hugged him tight and cried in his ear "I LOVE YOU RAHUL, I am really stupid to search for love everywhere when you, the love of my life is right in front of me. But now I realized it, no one can love me more than you, you are the only person who knows my true self and who never left me, I love you, Rahul. I know, I have done so many stupid things in the past, do you still love me?"

He hugged me tighter and said "what are you, a dummy? There wasn't a moment that I didn't love you" he pulled me out of the hug and he kissed me...

And that's how I frantically confessed...

The next day, college was nothing less than a press conference for me and why not, it's the 7th day and the whole college wants to know if I got a new boyfriend or not, I walked into the college with confidence and entered my classroom, soon Aman arrived and he stood in front of my desk and questioned me "So, did you find your perfect boyfriend yet?" and I answered with a smirk "I did!!! in fact, there is no one more perfect than him." Hearing that Aman's face turned red, he fumed "Who is he?" and then Rahul entered our classroom and screamed "It's me!!! And from now onwards mind your tone with Anjali, she is not your girlfriend to abuse and shout at!!" I was amazed by the power Rahul had, the whole class went silent, he came to me, grabbed my hand, and took me to the cafeteria. The fact that Rahul is better than Aman in every aspect made me happier, I was really happy and Rahul knew it, but my head was filled with lot of questions and I asked him "If you already knew, you are the one to me then why did you allow me to be in a relationship with Aman?, Why didn't you confess your feelings earlier?" he chuckled for a second and answered me "some things are meant to be felt by heart, those can only be understood through experience, Anjali!" That's true though, life is all about learning from experiences it may be good or bad, these experiences make the best stories. I am Anjali and this is my story...

ARIJITA CHAKRABARTI

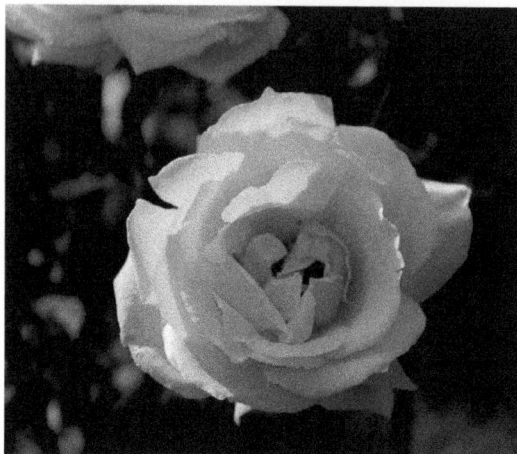

Arijita Chakrabarti was born in The City of Joy, Kolkata, India. She is a sophomore. She believes that "No matter what you are going through in your life you will surely see sunlight at the end of the tunnel only if you believe in you".

theworldthatlies@IG

Best Friends Forever

A photograph isn't just a picture it's an emotion, a feeling and a connection, the connection is the bridge which keeps our heart beating as one, the button that fills up all the unbuttoned pieces of our friendship. The love that acts as the strings to prevent our friendship from tearing apart. Our albums are bundles of memories tangled together in a beautiful inseparable mess and I know that even if I search the whole wide world I won't get such a caring, loving and loyal friend.

You are the staff on which I lean on when everyone turns their back. Sure, like all friendships our one is not perfect but it sure is one of the most cherished one in both our minds. We have had our fights but that is what keeps this bond so strong and so close. We have shared bitter tears and the brightest and sweetest of smiles. I feel at a loss of words to describe sometimes how paranoid I feel thinking that what will happen if our friendship trips over the edge, what if I lose my support on which almost all of my life depends? I am so sure that it will cause me to trip and fall on every step drowning me deeper and deeper into the mysterious cruel layers of life. So, thank you, for all the countless hours you have spent listening to me wail about my life.

Though we don't talk every day or get to see each other, I know that I will have you to grasp on whenever life pushes me down into a ditch or takes away the air necessary for me to breathe. I don't get to say this to you every day and so I am taking this opportunity to show how much you mean to me. No matter where life leads us in our future, I promise today that I will always stay in touch with you. You mean a lot to me as I know you are not my best friend but my sister separated by blood.

Revelation

Remember? That time we were 5 years old you had come rushing into my room blood violently pounding through your veins and your eyes were blood shot and as tears rolled down your soft pinkish cheeks I patted your back to calm you down. I had said that this inevitable feeling of loss would soon perish. However, I was like a sick little puppy trying to comfort another of my kind but little did you know that all the while I was comforting you my own heart was pounding against my chest and back then, I did not even know what that meant.

That time we were 10 years old playing our most favourite game I had scratched my knee really bad and I remember, you had torn a piece of your shirt sleeve and tied it around my knee, as you bent down tying it I could feel your soft hands brushing against my leg. For the same you had gotten a serious thrashing from your dad for the torn shirt sleeve yet you had silently borne all of it for the sake of our friendship.

Days became weeks, weeks became months and finally as months changed to years, our Friendship became stronger and stronger. Whenever you would miss your mother you would sneak into my room through the window and we would spend the whole night talking about all the blur pages of your mind about your mother. I still clearly recall your father humiliating you and indirectly me about how you could be a boy and shed tears in front of me and you had said that he would never know as he could not even keep your mother close. Even though you accepted me as the best person to confide in all your little secrets there was a part of me that was totally hidden from you.

As I grew up to become 15 years of age all the feelings that had been haunting me ever since you became my best friend became sorted and I knew exactly what I had been feeling. That day as you came back to my room and propped yourself up in my bed and shed those silent tears, once again you were unable to see or hear my loud wails. I know I could have told you but I was afraid that if I did maybe our friendship would break down to fragments and I couldn't afford it because this was the only thing that I treasured more than anything but the feeling was eating up my soul. So maybe I will never be able to tell this to you face to face so if you are reading just know that you are the one for whom my heart skips a beat every now and then. I know that recently I have been distancing myself from you and if you're okay with the fact that I have fallen hard for you please come back and allow me to hug you like you never left your place.

Remember?

Can you recall? That day after hearing the news my eyes welded up and my whole world cracked. However, you did not come to console me as you knew that the truth was so harsh that consolation couldn't be provided. That day we could not escape reality as the truth did not provide us with an escape. We had not been friends for a very long time yet the time we were together are the most carefully cherished memories of mine. However, like everything in life this friendship also drifted apart soon after you left.

Distance has drifted us apart. Distance has engulfed the invisible connection. Every day's busy life is just an excuse to prevent getting upset from the memories of the good old days. The two people who used to have millions of topics to talk about have run out of topics to talk. The hour calls have reduced to five minutes. Sometimes, the invincible urge to run away from this tedious life and go over childhood memories with you is unbearable but that is when my mind pings a notification saying "This is real world with no happily ever after".

We surely have been able to mix in our daily lives but I don't know about you but my heart very often aches to spend time with you like before. With every day that passes, I become a little okay with the fact that we may lose connection in the future. Though I may not know what the future holds for me, you or anyone, I know that no matter where I am or where I go I will always remember the memories which will stay lemon fresh like they took place just yesterday.

I don't know when I will talk to you again but remember that this message was not to blame you or me as the incident was no one's fault. It was FATE. This is just a reminder of how much I still care for you and I still am ready to look out for you. This is a mere note proving how much you still mean to me and how much I still love you.

YOGITHA SUBASH

She is yogitha, she is from Hyderabad, the city of pearls. she is a 90's kid, Grown up in a middle-class family.. she is a kind of introvert,& she prefers to stay at home rather than partying with her friends.. Even though she is from Hyderabad she doesn't like Hyderabadi biryani which is the famous food of her city.. Writing was always been a passion to her, what all she writes is based on her personal experience it's not just a thought, it's her emotions which she pen's it...That's all about her..

Yogitha_subassh@IG

A Letter To A Person Who Made Me Fall In Love Again

Have you ever met a person who changed your life? who made your world beautiful. who made you realise what exactly Love feels like? who taught you what unconditional love is. It might sound crazy unconditional love and all. But yes that's what exactly happened with me. I dint know swiping right on tinder will be a life changing thing to me. I met you as a stranger, who turned out to be the Love of my life. It was love at first sight. when I saw you I dint had second thought I just fell for you. I fell for you for the person you are. Your positive attitude gives me positivity, your calm nature tells me how to control my emotions & loving you gives me the ability not only to love you but also to love me. Unlike others your love doesn't make me weak, you make me strong and more confident.. whenever I look at you I see hope, belief and love. You make me sad and happy at the same time. Happy because you are in my life and sad because you don't love me back but not loving me back doesn't lesser my love for you.

I have learned that it's not what you have in your life, but who you have in your life counts. Though I don't expect anything from you, but I secretly wish that you should choose me. I know forever is a myth but I want to prove forever is Real. I need you to believe in the love in me, when am trying to prove my love for you. I really can't afford to lose you not because I love you but because am worried that nothing else will ever feel like love again after you.

I know you can't be my destiny, maybe I don't deserve a person as precious as you. may be Life has some other plans for us.

Though we don't share any relationship with each other but it's still you who I choose over everything and everyone else. I was wise enough to fall for you, But I hope am not a fool to let you Go. Confessing Our love to someone takes a lot of courage but you showed me that Love is something not just to be said but also to be shown.. I might not feel the same way tomorrow as I feel today but you will always be my Heart's Desire which I will cherish FOREVER...

AGHARTA

At twenty-two, Agartha dreams to become a poet and a writer. To find the words fitting perfectly in the blank pages of a book like a canvas waiting to be painted or a puzzle being deciphered. Agartha wants to someday wish to published her own book but too afraid for what comes after.

agharta05@IG

Loving You

Under the moonlit sky and sea of stars, he got down on one knee. His eyes were blue as the ocean, and captivating eyes mesmerized her sanity.

Then he uttered, "Will you marry me?"

Dumfounded and paralyzed — she was speechless while all eyes were on her.

"YES or NO!" she screamed at herself silently.

Nothing came out of her lips, but she tasted bitterness on her tongue. Heaven or hell — she chose to run away from all her fears.

She waited for his arrival to rescue her from her demons, but he didn't. He died of a broken heart.

Seascape

daylight gone to sleep

the sun hides from the horizon

while the moon's beauty

reflects on the crystal sea

a siren sung an untold story

of a love once found but lost

out of sight but etched in

the depths of the blue

her sad heart listened

to the music it weaves

for her one true love

while the sky cried for her

Kiss Of Death

the blood moon rise

after a hundred years of sleep

at twelve midnight

when he awoke from death

heartless in misery

no shadows cast in the dark

a slayer waits for his return

wreaking havoc in her thoughts

yet, the only chaos befalls her

—   his love

Lovestruck

thunder strikes
when cupid travels

his bow and arrows
to pierce lonely hearts
into falling in love

on his way to
the land of red
he fell asleep

a twinge of pain
on his chest

as he arises
his heart beats
for a love that's
never meant

heaven cried
when he fell in despair
trapped in cold rage

Betwixt

magic turns a frown into smiles

while a curse cast in chaos

a little girl wore a black cloak

while a little boy plays in heaven

she met him — then he met her

in between good and evil

her wings battered painted in crimson red

while his coated in gold and silver

forbidden love blossoms

yet, they didn't care

VENUS

love matches

mysteriously

"Good morning & Good night!"

Venus stays awake

to bake sweet cakes

add a little bit of spice

and a lot of love

sun came and moon left

hearts shattered and broken

love matches

mysteriously

Venus —

       "Why not him?"

DR. SATYAKI GIRI

Dr. Satyaki Giri is an up-and-coming dentist. A travel bug introvert who likes to collect books over humans. Writing hobby since school days.

satt_is_a_wallflower@IG

Fair-ish

Luna, the curious girl would watch in awe as the mysterious man of the high castle would set beautiful birds flying away, the view of which set ablaze the sunset sky.

It happened every day, no one else in the village would bat an eye over it, but she was broken from loss, left lonely by friends, and had the time to fantasize about everything, including that stranger.

Imagination in one's head never leaves one lonely. Whilst healing from the shattering sickness, she'd imagine him as a friend, one who can always amaze and never disappoints.

The day came, when Luna was enough to walk on her feet. Full of glee and rejuvenated enthusiasm, the first decision she took was to climb the hill. Eagerness and curiosity made her able to cross the line used to be drawn by the villagers over and over again.

The air outside smelt of sweaty independence. By day's break, she reached the castle. No one stopped her, asked about her or welcomed her. The vast castle yard was beautiful but ruined, reeking of a strange unfathomable sadness. What seemed like a man's shadow waved at her from top of the tower. She couldn't see his face, but followed the rocky steps towards nevertheless.

The approaching dusk seemed moody. Luna kept her distance and looked around upon reaching the top. A broken yet gentle voice reached her, 'You really think I could be your friend?'.

Reddened with pleasant surprise, she asked, 'How'd you know unless you try?' "Fair enough', it was a man's long suppressed laughter no doubt, 'Now that you've come this far...'

Facing the setting sun reddening the whole canvas, the man opened his chest like a cage, and let out a loud cry of agony. At the moment she didn't know, if it was real. As bloods seemed to be dripping, winged ugly bat-like minions started storming outside in the open sky. Shocked and awed, she forgot what happened next.

When she woke up, Luna found herself in her house's lawn, alone and facing the starry night sky. Partly scared, partly confused as memories came flooding in, she didn't know if it was a dream or reality. But, she knew she saw pain and someone was opening his heart. Real or magical, something was familiar about it. She made up her mind, she'll be going there again.

A smile twinkled the brightest facing the stars.

Dreams

Someone sprinkles the bliss of springs

Over our fragile bodies showering

From under the cracked feathers of strength

Watch as through the glass slide

The brilliant unknown

The magic that disappears when I stumble

On the top of my ground of glee

Surrounding the murmur of drowning incoherence

We are a song

Clad in the throbbing of the light

Decorating the ashen ground of white mess

We are a bunch of hope

Wings waiting eagerly.

SHRAVANI PRADEEP BARAVKAR

Shravani Pradeep Baravkar is budding writer at Spectrum of thoughts for the anthology "Sleight of hands".She is former student of BSc(comp.sci) and is currently studying BA(English).She hails from Pune,Maharashtra.Her hobbies include singing,drawing.

writeups_by_shravani@IG

Being magic

Sunlight beamed through my window,

splattering colours on my walls...

like nature's spending spree,

and I don't know if I exist

in all this magic around,

or the magic exists within me.

I see glory in all the flaws,

as I myself am flawed,

I don't get meshed in the appearance,

I plunge deep into the meaning,

behind the facade.

But many times, I feel as if I'm drowning, sometimes casted away,

I'm sure I'll wallow in this dive,

and will learn to float one day.

And even after falling in depths of misery

I'll be in acme of contentment someday,

cause although hope is a monster,

she still makes world less Gray.

So, beauty, blooms and blossoms

are always sprinkled everywhere for me,

since I know this is magic...magic is me.

Making miracles

I know I'm saying this a thousandth time...

I don't know how to make poems rhyme,

I don't get how people write

novels, books and skits,

Cause when I try to write something,

even my thinking works in bits.

I don't know how people use these soulful words and insightful metaphor,

Cause when I try to stitch

some letters together,

they just make my head sore.

I don't get how artists have this

lucidity of thoughts,

while I don't have a clue,

I sit blank in corner for hours,

mending my broken language

together with some glue.

So, I'll say it one more time,

I really don't know how to make poems rhyme,

But I do know it's a deed of broken hearts,

so romantic yet so tragic,

it's called making miracles, it is magic.

YEDDANAPUDI DEEPIKA

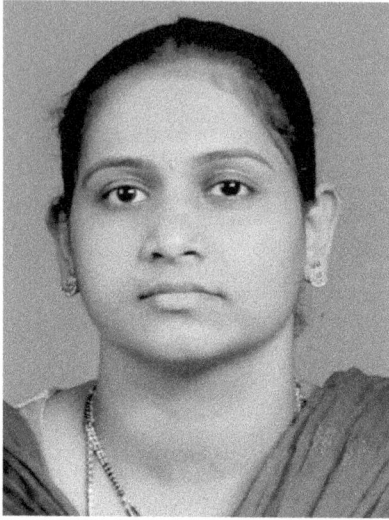

Yeddanapudi Deepika is a passionate poetess, a tech-savvy and a facilitator by profession.

Magical Gubbins

Lying silently in the corner of the room,

When teased with a wand, it goes zoom,

Look! there goes the broom, Vroom! Vroom!

Abracadabra, Gili - Gili choom,

Wave your wand and then you hum,

Ask for anything, here it comes.

Stinky socks, nail and fur,

In they go and then you stir,

Finally, the potion to the bottle we transfer.

Cloak, hat and a wand in hand,

A lousy cat to run your errand,

With your good deeds you become a legend.

A Wand in my hand

A wand in my hand,

With me it has a bond,

Always ready to respond,

To my every command.

A wand in my hand,

I can make things come true,

For me and you,

Believe it or not it is true.

A wand in my hand,

I consider myself to be Potter,

Do not think I am mad as a hatter,

I can make your teeth chatter.

A wand in my hand,

I consider myself to be Hermione Granger,

Always going to the rescue of someone in danger,

Even if he or she is a stranger.

A wand in my hand,

I consider myself to be Ron Weasley,

None should take me easily,

I am not silly.

A wand in my hand,

All the evil from this world, I will erode,

And make it a better abode,

A thousand-fold.

YEDDANAPUDI JEYAN

Yeddanapudi Jeyan is a poet and an author with inborn creative writing talent.

Magic and Gobbledygook

Harry potter is like the mascot of magic

Because he hasn't done anything tragic.

70 litres of dragon heart oil,

And with some magical jelly, you can make 7 elves who toil.

6 millilitres of a witch's blood,

And with some lemons, you can make the city flood.

Find some ear wax candles,

And with some potions, you can make fairy castles.

Find some polar bear fur,

And with some ginger, anything you can blur.

Find a young chap's eye,

And with some marble, you can make an invisible tie.

Find a tear of a frog,

And with some fish paste, you can make someone a hog.

Find an octopus's tentacle,

And with some glass, you can make an extra ventricle.

Find a small rock,

And with some cotton, you can make a talking croc.

Find a frozen duck,

And with some silicon, you can make a flying truck.

If I was a wizard,

Like Voldemort I won't make a blizzard.

Magic and fun together,

Can make the world as light as a feather.

The legend of Qwertia

There was a valley, far, far away,

Of art and dance, there was an array.

The valley was peaceful and calm,

It was full of charm.

Qwerty, was its name,

It was known for its fiery game.

Its people weren't lame,

But they were tame

But then came Irtes, an evil wizard,

Who turned everyone just for fun, into a lizard?

When everyone was confused,

By Irtes, they got bruised.

Everyone he teased,

And no one was pleased

When everyone was clueless,

The hero was flawless.

His name was Clifford,

He came to the valley when everyone suffered.

Clifford used magic to restore peace,

He defeated Irtes, with ease.

He defeated Irtes's Dragon,

And his Kraken.

He built his own lair,

He treated everyone with kindness and care.

Between Irtes and Clifford, there was an epic battle,

And Clifford broke the former's shuttle.

He was crowned the king of Qwertia,

But he went back to his home, Telletia.

AASHNA BHARGAVA

Aashna Bhargava is a student from Chandigarh with quite a lot on her mind. She uses poems and music as an escape from the usual chaos of life. She thoroughly enjoys a candle lit, incense filled atmosphere with a side of a cup of herbal tea in her free time.

apieceofmy__mind@IG

Imagination

A glance at you

my face lights up

the winds change direction impromptu

lightning surges up and down my spine

i smile at you wide

as tears roll down my cheeks

i never see you smile back

i never see you

was i only imagining?

Half Of Me

I'll give you half of me

the half I've been saving for myself

the half i loved the most

the rest are pieces and ashes

of a broken and burnt rose

with shattered and scattered thorns

i wouldn't want your hands tainted as well

Thoughts

It feels like something in me just broke into pieces

a million shards, its going to be a mess

trying to gather and rearrange them all

the blood and tears are going to make it worse

but you won't be here to help me with it

you're too busy, laughing and talking

I can't afford to disturb your happiness

but I thought you were all mine

Only A Reflection

Oh! It would be a blessing, you and me

if only you were mine

to hold my hand, to stroke my back,

to say it's alright, or perhaps it's going to be.

At this moment, nothing amuses me,

nor does anything excite.

Nothing but your presence by my side.

It's too bad you're only a reflection in the mirror.

-cherry

THE END

For contacting publication, VISIT:

Website:- www.sotpublication.com

Instagram:- https://www.instagram.com/spectrum.of.thoughts/

Linkedin:- https://www.linkedin.com/company/spectrum-of-thoughts

Twitter:- https://twitter.com/spectrumpublish

Ingram Content Group UK Ltd.
Milton Keynes UK
UKHW040848280323
419292UK00004B/186

9 789354 529030